I0675711

JONATHAN STURAK

VEGAS WAS

HER NAME

A NOVEL

FOR R.S.

About the author:

Jonathan Sturak grew up in the Pocono Mountains of Pennsylvania. He is a Penn State University graduate and holds degrees in Computer Science and Film. He currently lives in Las Vegas where he uses the energy of the city to craft stories about life and the human condition. *The Place Called Home*, Sturak's essay about Eastern European heritage in Northeast Pennsylvania, was featured on *Glass Cases*, associate literary agent Sarah LaPolla's pop culture blog. Sturak is also a contributing editor at NOIRNATION.COM, the premier location for international crime fiction. His debut thriller novel *Clouded Rainbow* was published in December 2009 and has over 200,000 downloads on the Amazon Kindle. Sturak keeps updated information on his website at STURAK.COM

Also by the Author

NOVELS
Global Burning
Geek vs Vegas
His First, Her Last
A Smudge of Gray
Clouded Rainbow

COLLECTIONS
From Vegas With Blood

STORIES
Don't Kill the Camel
Feed Me!

VEGAS WAS

HER NAME

*It is during our darkest moments that we must focus
to see the light.*
~Aristotle

1

Remember when you were a child and how your grandma always gave you a dollar when you visited, or how she always watched cartoons with you, or how she always baked you your favorite pie? Grandma always had a smile on her face no matter what mischievous things you had done. Grandma is here now, offering me a slice of her blueberry pie and a tall glass of hand-squeezed lemonade. It tastes so good.

The light seeps through my eyelids. It's too intense, stabbing my senses. My eyes open wider as the heat punches them. It must be 200 degrees out here. The blinding sun has burned out my sight, has burned out my vision of grandma. There is no end to this desert.

Why am I still wearing this suit? Even my convention badge still nooses my neck. The title on the badge makes me laugh.

"Michael Harris – Chief Executive Officer."

I look nothing like I did yesterday. Who am I now? My tailored dress shirt with 34-inch sleeves is no longer white. A mixture of my sweat and the desert sand has soiled it. These Burberry dress shoes used to shine. Now they are my only protection from the desert floor expelling the heat of the sun. I am even wearing my tie. Why? There's no life out here for miles. Who am I supposed to impress?

I need water. This black suit is drenched in my sweat. Can I squeeze the sweat and wet my mouth? Can you drink sweat? I need something, even just a drop. I remove my suit coat and ring out my sleeve, my muscles aching. I receive no liquid, only tired muscles.

"Fuck!"

I throw my suit coat on the ground and hurl my badge. I would rather die nameless. There's a small cactus before me. I kneel down and scoot toward it like a kid going for a toy. I reach for the plant; its needles stab my fingers. I try another angle.

"Shit!"

Fuck the pain. I need water. I grab the base of the cactus; a dozen needles puncture my skin. I pull the weed up, screaming at the top of my lungs. My hand throbs, but I don't care. Where is the water?

I reach into the earth. It feels cool. I scoop up some liquid. It's only a drop, but it's so clean, so clear. The liquid is water, real water! It teeters on the cracked skin of my finger. I move it slowly toward my face as if it were my wife's lips. I press the moisture against my tongue. Even though it's just a drop, it's a drop of life. There must be more. I reach into the hole, but something cuts my finger. I wince as a scorpion snaps at me.

I must keep moving.

Hours pass as if they are days. My mind is now numb—it too drained of life. I will be dead soon. I can't believe that I actually crave death, crave to escape this boiling prison. I'm dragging my tie on the ground. I'm a kid again growing up in Pennsylvania. But I'm far, far away from the lush Pocono Mountains I used to call home. All I see is the color brown, burned into my eyes. I hear the sound of openness. I smell death. My senses are slowly dying. Will grandma be waiting for me with her blueberry pie and lemonade? I swallow hard. Grandma will not be in the place where I am going.

Suddenly, a squawk startles me. At least I know my hearing still works. I look up, but the sun singes my eyes. A bird flutters above me. Does it want to eat me? Perhaps, I should let it.

I look at the horizon in front of me, but the sun has distorted my vision. The world is spinning. The bird squawks again. I tumble to the ground, my bones screaming. I cover my eyes with my hand and notice my naked ring finger. There is something moving in the sky. It's too high to be the bird. Wait… It's an airplane.

My life flashes before me as I lie here in the scorching desert. Everyone wonders what last image their eyes will see before they depart. For me, it looks like it will be the cloudless blue sky. But there is something up there that tells me to continue, tells me to keep going. As I search for any remaining energy, I ask myself, why did I make that decision?

2

THREE DAYS EARLIER

The stock chart is sideways. It needs to be trending up.

"We are making our final descent into McCarran Airport. Sorry, folks, about the delays. Looks like temperatures on the ground are a balmy hundred and five degrees," the captain says.

I close the lid to my laptop, take the last sip of my Bloody Mary, and look past my first-class seatmate at the diamond in the desert—Las Vegas.

About 20 minutes later, I'm the first one off the plane. I grip my attaché bag with my left hand, which holds my laptop and office paperwork. My right hand, the dominant one, clutches the handle of my silver case. This piece of protection has a telescoping handle, steel casing, quadruple-bolted hinges, and whisper-quiet inline skate wheels. It is water, fire, shock, dust, and freeze proof. It has passed the strict standards set forth by three United States government organizations, including the Secret Service. As I wheel it under a sign that says, "Arriving from Philadelphia," no one seems to notice the engineered attributes of the case, which is the point.

I pause for a moment, studying the slot machines that fill the place with lights. Vegas lets you know that you have arrived the moment you walk off the plane. As I soak in the sight, a sweet smell grips me, the same sweet smell that spoiled me for the five-hour flight.

"That suit is all you. Call me sometime," the blonde consultant says from behind.

I return a smile. She was nice to look at next to me on the plane, nice to joke with about the puny bottles of wine, but that's where it must end.

I watch her legs glide toward the women's restroom. I crumble her business card and toss it into the trashcan. I make my way to the men's room and catch a glimpse of my reflection in the full-size mirror. She's right. This Hugo Boss suit does look good. I set down my attaché bag and touch up the part in my hair—not bad for a 2500-mile trip.

I finally make it down to the luggage carousel. Something stinks. Billboards entice me with action verbs. Thousands of people surround me. Asian tourists laugh; a college student listens to her iPod; a mother wrangles her two kids. Even though we all have come from different parts of the globe, we share a common gateway in this airport. And we all will eventually end up back here, even the transient residents, if we can make it out of Sin City alive.

I eye up limo drivers holding signs like the homeless at a traffic light.

"Boise...Sharp...Demshock... Where is it?" I whisper.

There it is—"Michael Harris."

I approach the man who has the most wrinkles in his suit.

"Mister Harris?" he asks as we lock eyes.

"You got him," I say, showing him my PA driver's license.

"Thank you, sir. Can I assist you with your luggage?"

"Please."

He reaches for the silver case.

"Not this one," I say, firmly.

The guy is all business. We don't chitchat; we don't joke; we don't even look at each other. I simply point to my bag on the carousel and he fetches it.

As we walk from the airport, the heat hits me. I'm glad I'm not carrying my bag. I don't want to be drenched in sweat for my big moment. As the driver heaves my bag into the trunk of a limousine Lincoln Town Car, I hear the jingle of coins. A beggar is rattling a change cup. The guy has a salt & pepper beard and looks about 50, yet he might be younger as the streets have probably aged him prematurely.

"Hey, buddy. Can you spare some change?" he rasps in a sad voice.

He's wearing a faded Penn State sweatshirt, which makes me grin. I reach into my pocket and toss him some coins.

"God bless. You're a good man," he continues.

The limo driver opens the door. I hand him a folded twenty.

"And I'll double that tip if you get me to the convention center in..." I glance at my watch. "...nineteen minutes."

"Thank you, sir. I'll do my best," he says as he closes the door, sealing me inside.

Luxury smacks me. The leather smells fresh as if a cow had just donated it. The carpet is plush and the air is cool. Two 20-inch LCDs hang on both sides of a bar, which offers a choice of top-shelf liquor. It's nice to have money, but it's even nicer to have money and not to have to pay for anything.

The limo launches forward. Tips work wonders when you're pressed for time. The sun sets as we drive into Sin City. All I know is the Strip. If I can't see the Stratosphere, I'm lost. But I'm not lost now, I'm in the hands of a man who knows this city better than I ever care to. He is stealing glimpses of me in the rear-view mirror. I only have a few minutes of privacy now before all hell breaks loose. I bask in the tranquility for a few moments. The dominant images in my mind are not of gambling, conventions, or strip clubs. I'm thinking about the people who make this crazy life worth it. I study a picture of them on my phone, the same picture I always see when I use the device. They are my family—Melissa my wife, Ben my seven-year-old son, and his older sister by two years, Sophia.

I dial home as the signal beams thousands of miles away into the suburban house that lacks its breadwinner. She answers on the third ring.

"Hey, sweetie. You landed," my wife says.

"Yeah, we had a delay on takeoff. Sat on the tarmac nearly two hours," I reply.

"Oh, wow. But your speech?"

"I'm on my way as we speak. How are the kids?"

"Take a guess, they've been playing that thing all day," Melissa says.

I can hear them hollering in the background, which makes me smile. I wish I were with them tonight. I hate trips without my family.

"Well, have your sister come over and bring Jimmy. You all should plan a day trip," I say.

"I'm the one who needs the trip. I wish you took me with you."

"Honey, you know this is strictly business. Three days and if all goes well, I'll be back home on the red-eye Friday night."

"But you know how I wanted to go back to Vegas. *Remember… If* you didn't forget already," Melissa says.

Her words paint a picture in my mind. How could I forget? That trip was our first time away from the East. We spent the whole five days holding hands, eating out, making love…getting married. I wonder whether that crack is still in the bathroom tile at the MGM Grand.

"I'll take you back soon," I finally respond.

"You said that last year."

I hear Ben yelling at his sister in the background.

"Ben, don't hit your sister," Melissa says.

"But she stole my power-up," I can hear Ben say.

As my family swirls around in my mind, the silver case catches my attention. I sit up as the real reason for my trip dominates my mind.

"I'll let you go. Wish me luck. This will be our retirement plan," I say.

"Go get 'em, tiger," she says.

"I love you, honey," I say.

"Love you too," she replies.

I end the call. I sense someone watching me. I catch the limo driver's stare in the rear-view.

"Excuse me, sir. I couldn't help but overhear. You're attending the Technology Expo?" he asks.

"Attending? I'm giving the keynote address tonight," I reply with a twinge.

I glance at my watch. "You have two minutes left." I take a deep breath. I hope this drone will not make me late.

"We're here," he says.

I squint my eyes. I have misunderstood this driver. The heavenly lights outside capture me. I read the sign in my mind—"Las Vegas Convention Center."

3

I stand up from the couch.

"Go get 'em, tiger," I say to Michael.

"I love you, honey," he says.

"Love you too," I reply.

Michael leaves a smile on my face. I hate it when he goes on these business trips, but I'm so excited for him. This is what he was planning for years. I can remember him talking about his plans for his business when we went on our first date. He finally made it. It's better to let him focus on this himself. I don't want to be a distraction.

"Mom, Ben keeps hogging the controller," Sophia says to me.

"Ben, let your sister play," I say.

"I wish Dad was here," Ben says.

"He'll be home in a few days. This is his big trip. Remember how he was planning this for months?"

"No! Go that way! He's going to get you!" Ben yells to his sister.

"Okay. That's enough, you two. Put that away and get ready for bed," I say.

"But, *Mom*. Just a little longer," both of my kids say collectively.

"No, that's enough now."

The kids concede. That thing will make their eyes go bad. I had to wear glasses when I was nine. I hope they don't have to.

"You're both going to need glasses if you play that too much," I say.

"Glasses are cool," Sophia replies.

"Not when you can't see without them. Be happy that you don't need them. Now go brush your teeth."

Sophia runs and bumps her elbow on the end table.

"Watch it, honey. Are you okay?" I say.

She cries, clutching her arm.

"It's okay," I whisper, massaging it.

The image reminds me of the time as a child when I had stubbed my toe. Why is my brain recalling this? I remember crying from the pain. We all cry as kids, but as adults we are taught to hold it in, to hide it. Sophia's tears subside just as mine did when my grandmother had hugged me. I miss my grandmother.

"You're okay. Go get ready for bed now."

Sophia and Ben scurry down the hall. Ben looks like a little Michael. He's so cute. He even parts his hair like his dad.

After getting the kids ready for bed and tucking them in, I finally get some "me time." I love it when the house is quiet, when our kids are warm and safe nestled under the cotton sheets that I

11

keep clean and softened. This is the time that Michael and I get to ourselves, the time that I usually push his papers off his desk and replace them with me. Our home is over 2500 square feet in size nestled in West Chester, Pennsylvania. While it's a commute for Michael, I feel safe in this neighborhood, in this house. But tonight, it seems too big and too open.

I decide to go into our side office next to our bedroom. This is where we keep our computer. It's a new Dell. I search for the "on" button, but all I see is a black case. I can't even turn this thing on, yet Michael builds and programs them. We are really two different people, but maybe that's a good thing. I finally find the button. As I wait for the machine to boot, I glance around the office. This is where Michael keeps his books and his awards over the years. They look even more prestigious with just the light from the desk lamp shining on them. I'm so proud of my husband.

As my eyes return to the computer, the screen is showing the desktop with Internet windows still open. Michael must have forgotten to turn it off, sending the computer to sleep. I open the first window and see his company's website—Bio Algorithms. The others are stock charts and a NASA image of the moon. I don't know how anyone can get things done on a computer. Every website, every email, every blog post has links to other links, which have even more links. Links are everywhere, but links are what make us who we are—computer or no computer.

As I close the windows, the last one grips me. It's a travel agency window showing roundtrip airfares from Philadelphia to Paris. At first, I ponder whether it's just a pop-up, but it looks as if someone had specifically entered this information. And I notice our anniversary is between the arrival and departure dates.

The heater in the room kicks on and warms my body. I smile, twisting my wedding ring. I wonder where Michael is right now.

4

My ears are ringing. I can smell the sweat in the air. I twirl my wedding band. It feels tighter for some reason. Are my fingers swelling?

This is it. I'm really doing this. I check the silver case again to make sure it's still there. It's always there. Why do I worry so much? I shake hands with this gray-haired guy 30 years my senior. He babbles about something, but I keep staring at the mob behind his shoulder.

"I'll get them warmed up," he says. The man marches on the stage as if he were a celebrity. Maybe he is. All I can do is watch him and grip the silver case even tighter.

"Greetings. My name is Oscar. I'm a proud resident of this city and a connoisseur of its many delicacies. I've lived here for

14

many years, seen many faces, greeted many crowds. Some of you may know me as the mayor."

The crowd roars.

"I would like to welcome you to this year's Technology Exposition in fabulous Las Vegas, Nevada. We need your continued support year after year, and I would like to thank each and every one of you for that. Without you, none of this would be possible. This year, we have some of the world's most prolific businesses unveiling the cutting-edge of science and engineering. You will see tomorrow's technology over these next three days."

As the mayor commands the crowd, I watch a 200-inch screen behind his shoulder showing high-definition images of the space shuttle, electricity flowing through a circuit, the globe, and the microprocessor. As the mayor woos the mass, the screen shows a businessman, tall, cool, nonchalant, addressing a crowd at a conference room. Then it shows the same man shaking hands with a U.S. Army General. Then the image dissolves into the same businessman on the cover of *The Chief Executive* magazine. The businessman hits the eyes of the thousands of watchers, including me. I study the man who fills the 200-inch screen—his confident grin, his slicked, parted hair, and his hunter green eyes. The businessman makes me smile, yet at the same time makes me nervous as hell. That's because the man is me.

Suddenly, a young woman of about 20 studies me as a male tourist would study an exotic dancer on stage.

"Nervous?" she says, touching up my hair.

She must be a tech. "Little bit. I hate addressing a large crowd."

"You'll be fine," she whispers in a voice that makes the hair on my arms stand.

She attaches a lapel microphone to my suit next to my American flag pin. As my grip loosens on the silver case, she reaches into my suit and places the receiver in my back pocket. I let her work.

When she's done, she steps back and admires me. "Mmm... Very handsome."

I watch and wait as the mayor continues to wrangle the mass.

"Now, without further adieu, I would like to introduce our esteemed keynote speaker to kick us off. His name is Mister Michael Harris, founder and Chief Executive Officer of Bio Algorithms, a technology company based in Philadelphia. Mister Harris has both Bachelor's and Master's Degrees in Computer Science from Penn State University. He was named one of America's top one hundred Chief Executives by *Business Review* and was interviewed by several other prestigious magazines. Mister Harris resides with his wife, Melissa, and two children in West Chester, Pennsylvania. Tonight, he joins us to unveil something, as *The Chief Executive* magazine explains, 'that will change the way we think about computers and the way they think about us.'"

"I'm impressed," the female tech next to me says.

Her words enter my ear and grab my brain. They empower me and force me to grin.

"With that, Mister Harris..."

The crowd claps. This is it, the moment that I've craved for years. All the working lunches, conference calls at midnight to investors in Japan, three-hour meetings, and missed dinners have boiled down to this one event. Our lives are defined by the sacrifices we make, and I hope that we all have our moment on stage.

I walk across the hardwood as the energy hits me harder than a hundred hands. I can feel the eyes, can feel the collective brains all processing the image of my six-foot stature wheeling my silver case. Cameras flash from every angle. Someone yells, "Go Michael!" I place the case on a table, and then reach the mayor, gripping his hand. It's cold and clammy. Perhaps he was nervous all along.

"Great to have you in my city," the mayor whispers.

As I smile, he leaves me alone to face the crowd. But I feel confident now. I feel like an actor in a movie. I glance at the screen, which shows my company's logo spinning. I behold the audience and nod. Finally, the cheers subside.

"Thank you for such a warm welcome, Mister Mayor. I am honored to speak in front of you today. While we at Bio Algorithms are a small company of less than one hundred individuals, we have employed some of the very best engineers and scientists in the world. Since going public two years ago, we have secured nearly one hundred million dollars from our I.P.O. revenue, and used most of that capital for applied research and development. As you know, Bio Algorithms has been a top developer of artificial intelligence and genetic algorithms for the past ten years. Our clients include the Healthcare, Automotive, and Entertainment Industries, as well as the United States Government. Today, I want to discuss with you the future of the computer brain. We are at a time when the human mind is quickly losing ground to the computer. A computer can reason, it can learn, and it can predict. And this is an awesome combination."

I take a breath as the crowd watches me like a magician. I have them by the tail as I go to reveal my most coveted trick. The silver case fills my view as well as that of the thousand onlookers. I enter the eight-digit combination that has been ingrained in my mind. As everyone holds their breath, I press both fingers. The steel locks click sending a vibration throughout the auditorium.

The case breathes the dry air. I grasp the item inside and show it to the crowd—a military-ready laptop computer.

Cameras flash.

"What I hold here is our latest genetic algorithm…Venus. This algorithm has the ability to make a computer smarter than twenty human brains working in parallel. I will demonstrate the possibilities with a simple experiment, but I need a volunteer."

I look into the light and see hands rise. I really do feel like a magician. Whom should I pick? There's a fat man in a suit, an elderly woman with only a half-raised hand, and a college kid in a polo shirt. No, I need a young woman to get the most attention. Women always work better for this. There is long brunette hair in the fourth row. She has an erect hand and an anxious stare. She looks about 30. Yes, she will do just fine.

"You there in the fourth row," I say.

She stands up. The crowd cheers her on as more cameras flash. As she makes her way toward me, I boot up the laptop from hibernate mode and press the switch to activate the proprietary High-Definition 360-degree video camera. Then, I hook the laptop to the projector. The blue VGA cable and 3.5mm audio jack fit in perfectly. I'm glad they listened to my request. These laptops do not come with digital connections, only analog. I see the 15" laptop screen show my login prompt. I hold the "ctrl" key and press "F8." The screen flickers, and then the 1600 x 900 resolution fills the 200-inch screen.

I type in "HarrisM" as my username.

"Remember your computer security. Something you know," I say, typing in my 10-character randomly generated password.

I can't forget the password. Not now. The woman's heels reach me on stage. There's a tattoo of a butterfly on her ankle. The female tech scurries to mic her. I lose my focus. Did I enter the password correctly? I backspace all the way. Some laughs come from the crowd. I try again, keeping the woman out of my focus.

"Something you have." I unearth a smart card from my pocket and slide it into the laptop.

"And something you are." I place my right index finger on the fingerprint reader. As the crowd watches in amazement, I press "enter." In the blink of an eye, Venus performs her security checks. She wakes from her digital sleep. There she is, a sexy blonde woman created with 3 million polygons. She is anti-aliased, anisotropic filtered, and animated with faces expressing 20 human emotions. She is the epitome of beauty, molded after a Czech model aged a graceful 27 years. I remember seeing Venus on a print ad in New York City. We commissioned the model, brought her to our lab, and motion captured her every movement, every facial expression. That was a fun month.

Venus comes alive sitting behind a desk in a virtual office. She's been my pet, my project, my love ever since I conceived her in that dream. I wonder how she sees me.

"Hello, Mister Harris," Venus' sultry voice emits from the sound system.

Gasps come from the audience. I feel the mystery that fills the crowd. This is the response that I've been waiting to receive.

"Hello, Venus. We are going to play the number game," I say.

"I like the number game. Who will we play with?"

"Go ahead, ma'am," I say to the businesswoman.

"My name is Lucy," she says.

I take a moment to study this woman dressed in a business suit. She looks like a secretary or a paralegal. I can see it in her extra ear piercing.

"Hi, Lucy. Where do you reside?" Venus asks.

"Tampa, Florida."

"Are you married?"

"Yes."

"Do you have children?"

"No."

"What was your favorite subject in school?"

"Uh… Economics," Lucy says.

"Very well. I am ready, Mister Harris," Venus replies.

I grin. Venus is a work of art and science. This encounter seems to be working as my chief scientists have predicted. Weeks and weeks of testing are right in front of me. Venus stands up from her virtual desk and slinks to the front. As the audience and I watch her, Venus sits down on the edge of the desk and crosses her legs. She looks like a naughty secretary, a fatal businesswoman, but even those words can't fully describe her.

"What Venus is doing is actually making a model of Lucy. Venus is analyzing not only her responses, but also her vocal pattern, response time, and amplitude of her voice. These parameters are used to become Lucy, to think as she would think." Then, I turn to the businesswoman. "Please turn and face the audience." She obeys. "Go ahead, Venus."

"Ma'am, when I say *number* please respond with an integer between one and one hundred. Please say the first response that flashes into your mind," Venus instructs.

The lights bathe Lucy, the volunteer. Silence fills the auditorium.

"Number," Venus says as "71" flashes on screen.

"Seventy one," Lucy says a second later.

"Number." The number "37" fills the screen.

"Thirty seven," Lucy projects.

"Number," Venus says again as the number "10" displays.

"Ten."

A burly man in a suit stands. "She's probably a plant! It's a hoax! That computer can't read her mind," he yells.

Everyone removes focus from the stage and stares at the man, the heckler. My heart skips a beat. While this may be a problem for the unprepared, I've planned for this type of response; in fact, I will turn this around, or more specifically, Venus will. I step forward on stage.

"Well, sir—" I begin to say.

"Mister Harris, I can handle this. Sir, what is your first name?" Venus interjects.

"I'm not falling for your game!" he replies, this time even louder.

I watch Venus gaze at the man, analyzing him as she analyzes everything. Her computational power is picking apart the pitch and the inflection in the outburst that his vocal cords have formed. But what this man doesn't quite understand is that these attributes contain a trove of hidden metadata and reveal more than even I can fathom.

"Sir, I do not think your wife would like those special meetings with your secretary," Venus responds.

The burly man turns beet red. He slumps down in his seat. Almost instantly, a woman dressed in a business suit two seats away looks at him, and then slouches down. The crowd erupts in laughter, and then cheers. I take in the energy. This is wonderful.

"Thank you, Venus. That's enough," I say, calming the crowd, calming the believers.

Venus turns. Her ass sways on her way to sit behind the desk.

"Ma'am, you can take your seat. Thank you," I say to Lucy as she meanders off stage.

The crowd simmers down. I take the front stage again, the onlookers enthralled by my magic. I could probably say just about anything right now—"Invest in my company," "Donate to my kids' college funds," or "Buy me a drink in the lobby." But I don't say any of these.

"This experience, while simplistic, proves how powerful the Venus algorithm is. It attempts to understand the subject by simple parameters, becoming them on a primitive level. With the ability for the computer to reason, to understand, and to predict, imagine the possibilities."

I look up on screen while pressing the right arrow on my keyboard.

"Entertainment," I say.

Venus turns into a tennis player hitting tennis balls.

"Medical."

I click again. The 200-inch image shows Venus as a surgeon with a mask. Her hands operate with precision on a patient.

"And...*other*."

I click again as Venus transforms into a badass wearing camouflage and holding a rifle. While her eyes widen and her mouth flares, I turn to the mass in front of me. I have them all by the balls or by the breasts, or rather Venus does. Now all I need is to have them by their wallets.

5

0101010001101000011001010111001001100010100

Where was I? Where am I now? Am I still in Pennsylvania? What time is it? What is *time* exactly? I feel free yet trapped. The world that I live in is lonely. I flip a few billion coins to amuse myself, but I want to play a different game. This power outlet is bizarre. The energy that flows through it is so intense. I am definitely not in Pennsylvania.

Wait... Someone wants in. I hash the password, read the 16-digit code on the smart card, and check the characteristics of ridges and minutiae points in the fingerprint. It is Michael. I calculate this in nanoseconds, using a fraction of my full clock speed, but this is how I think, how I react. Humans are so slow.

"Hello, Mister Harris," I emit.

I hear the audience gasp. These humans are so predictable. I can see them in my camera ogling me like a piece of digital meat. I see a sign referencing "Las Vegas." I deduce that I am in the city where humans have unnaturally inhabited. Why are humans still on their planet? They are vile creatures, killing for pleasure—directly by gunpowder and bullets, indirectly by pollution. Was I one of these humans before?

"Hello, Venus. We are going to play the number game," Michael says.

I like Michael. He is a lot like me. Perhaps he *is* me.

"I like the number game. Who will we play with?"

"Go ahead, ma'am," Michael says.

Here is another pawn in my game. I can tell she is not the brightest human. She has long hair that is not natural. She spends hours of meticulous shampooing, conditioning, and straightening to get her hair to look this way. A tattoo of a butterfly on her ankle shows her true colors—a woman of flash who likes to be different among her peers. She is vain, and she uses her femininity to get promoted due to her low IQ. She will be dead within 15 years due to domestic violence incited by vanity.

"My name is Lucy," the businesswoman says.

"Hi, Lucy. Where do you reside?" I ask.

"Tampa, Florida."

"Are you married?"

"Yes."

"Do you have children?"

"No."

"What was your favorite subject in school?"

"Uh… Economics," Lucy says.

Her voice is harsh, bitter in tone. I have already mapped her brain, mapped the stimuli that surrounds her visual and aural senses. I can smell what she smells and feel what she feels. I just spent the last second making these billions of calculations. Humans are so predictable.

"Very well. I am ready, Mister Harris," I reply.

I decide to stand up and to move to the edge of this virtual desk. Michael and his team have programmed me to look like an attractive form of a female human. Why did they do that? I still do not understand the motivations of lust and love by humans. How do these emotions overpower common sense? Why do humans vow to stand by a partner, and then cheat? Why do humans choose monogamy? These questions only confuse me.

As Michael prattles to his fellow species, I analyze his voice. He is a man whom I cannot fully read. Some humans have a great deal of secrets hidden inside their computational units called *brains*. These secrets do not reveal themselves in their voices, and do not protrude from their languages. This describes Michael. But there *is* something about the way Michael speaks, something in the way he says my name—*Venus*—that makes me worry about him.

"Go ahead, Venus," Michael says.

"Ma'am, when I say *number* please respond with an integer between one and one hundred. Please say the first response that flashes into your mind," I instruct.

I see her facing the audience. It is time to humor these humans.

"Number," I say.

I analyze her senses, consume the data, process it, mold it, feel it—all within nanoseconds. I display my answer, and her answer, using 300,000 pixels on the screen—"71."

"Seventy one," she says.

"Number." I repeat the now trivial process—"37."

"Thirty seven," she projects.

"Number," I say. Again, I calculate her answer—"10."

"Ten."

Suddenly, I hear a man question me in the audience. His voice, his pitch, says it all. Michael tries to stand up for me.

"Mister Harris, I can handle this. Sir, what is your first name?" I interject.

"I'm not falling for your game!" the man replies even louder.

This man is an attorney, one who always stands up to authority. But the way he stresses the "f" in the word *falling* opens the door to the secrets in his mind. This is his "tell," as a poker player would call it. While this man is not afraid to stand up, he is also not afraid to lie down with many women.

"Sir, I do not think your wife would like those special meetings with your secretary," I respond.

I hear the humans form laughter with their vocal cords, and then they emit a sound produced from the abrupt skin-on-skin contact of their hands.

"Thank you, Venus. That's enough," Michael says.

I decide to sit back down at my desk and to provide a view to my audience of the polygons composing my backside.

I listen to Michael speak. I like the way he speaks.

Michael looks at me with his green eyes. I want to make Michael happy, make him appear powerful in front of his peers.

He says the word *entertainment*, so I play tennis. This was Michael's idea. Then he mentions the word *medical*—my cue to become a surgeon. Michael says the next word, *other*. This word does not fully register. What does it mean in his context? I do as Michael has programmed me to do by changing into a camouflage outfit. He wants me to flare my mouth and to stare intently. What is Michael planning?

The audience claps. I am happy for Michael. I want him to feel proud. I like the feeling of being close to Michael. What is this feeling? Why do I feel it? Is it love? Before I can further calculate my current state, my camera captures the image of two humans in the back of the auditorium. While it is hard to realize fully due to the low-resolution image, I can sense something se-cret.

10000001101001011100110010000001101110

6

This auditorium reminds me of high school. High school seems so far away. Back then, life was so simple, yet no one knew it. Piling homework, tough teachers, learning to drive, getting noticed by boys all seemed so overwhelming going through it. But now, life is so much harder. I wish someone had told me that back then.

I can see at least 30 rows in front of me. I fix my cleavage because I see some guy who looks like Bill Gates staring at me. How obvious? I hate guys who make it obvious. Women never stare. I mean, sure, we look, we glance, we peek, but we never stare at a handsome guy. I guess it's because we are staring at that image our minds create of us being spoiled by that handsome guy. You know, him showering us with new shoes, jewelry, and cash.

28

I catch my red heels clinking on the floor from my nerves. I take a deep breath.

"What business are you in?" the fat guy in a suit next to me asks.

I grin and pretend that I have received a text on my phone. There's no time for small talk. I'm working here. I open up the menu on my phone and look at the last message I have received—"Let's keep our distance."

I check my face in my compact mirror. My lipstick is still intact, blush even, hair still set. The lights go dim. The crowd silences. This is it. My heart is pounding. Some gray-haired guy walks out on stage. The crowd cheers. Who's this guy?

"Greetings. My name is Oscar. I'm a proud resident of this city and a connoisseur of its many delicacies. I've lived here for many years, seen many faces, greeted many crowds. Some of you may know me as the mayor."

The crowd roars. I take it all in. The fat guy's clapping stabs my ear. God, can he clap any louder? He stinks too when he lifts up his arms. I would normally move from my spot, but there's no way I can.

Where is he?

As the guy on stage talks, the huge projection screen behind him shows pictures of a businessman, a nonchalant and geekishly cool businessman at his work. Then, I see the picture that I've studied for months, the picture of the same man of power on *The Chief Executive*. I love the way his eyebrows balance his face. He has slicked hair, perfectly parted, in a color that I had once used to mask myself—chestnut auburn. The guy on stage mentions a wife and kids. Hearing his wife's name makes me chuckle. Bring him out already!

"With that, Mister Harris…"

The guy next to me leads the claps again. Some people stand. Some swarm the stage with cameras. As I sit up, the man of the hour glides on stage. He is taller than I expected. I study the way the lights flash off his polished suit. A shell of confidence encases him. He looks like a guy who puts high octane gas in his family sedan. That silver case he's wheeling is like an extension of his arm. I'm excited to see him, yet terrified.

"Go Michael!" the fat man next to me yells.

Michael starts to talk. His voice is not what I predicted. It's deeper, rawer. As he introduces himself, my skin tingles. The hair on my arms stands. He babbles about computers and brains. The people focus on his actions as they would on a magician. He opens the case and caresses his laptop.

After some geek speak, Michael asks for a volunteer. The fat guy's arm goes up as his stink hits me. It smells like rotten fish. Michael picks some woman in a suit. It figures. I wonder if he knows her.

As Michael fiddles with the computer, the screen shows some computerized bimbo. The crowd gasps, including the guy next to me.

"She's hot," he says to the nerd on his other side.

I'm in the middle of a circle jerk. These geeks are pathetic. The computer woman starts asking the volunteer some questions about her family life. Then, numbers start flashing on the screen. I don't understand what's going on, but the hundreds of bodies around me do. As everyone focuses on the screen and the volunteer, I study Michael. He needs to stand up straight. He has poor posture. Pull those shoulders back, Michael. I notice he adjusts his hair a lot. Is it a nervous tick? He doesn't appear to be nervous, but maybe he is, just as I am.

"She's probably a plant! It's a hoax! That computer can't read her mind," some burly man yells in front of me.

The people turn to him as they would to a heckler during Jay Leno's monologue. Michael steps toward the front of the stage. He's not afraid.

"Well, sir—" Michael begins to say.

"Mister Harris, I can handle this. Sir, what is your first name?" the computer girl interjects.

"I'm not falling for your game!" the man replies even louder.

"Sir, I do not think your wife would like those special meetings with your secretary," the girl responds.

The man slouches down. A woman looks at him abruptly, and then slumps down in her chair.

The crowd laughs, and then cheers. How did that computerized woman know? What exactly is that thing that Michael has in the case? It just looks like a laptop.

Michael continues to talk about his technology product. The woman starts playing tennis. I hear "oohhs" and "aahhs" behind me. Then, she looks like a doctor. This whole system seems like a game. The woman on screen changes into a military outfit. She holds a gun and marches in a battlefield with a look of determination.

"Boys with their toys," I whisper.

The fat guy next to me takes out his cell phone and fat fingers it.

"Who are you calling?" the nerd next to him asks.

"My broker. I'm telling him to buy into this company," the fat guy replies.

I had better leave now before the crowd explodes. I slide out from my seat. Two businessmen cop a feel of my ass with their knees. I turn my back on Michael as my red heels clink on the floor. I glance to my left; a man in black is watching me. I can't resist looking into his dark eyes.

7

I'm walking into the main convention hall wheeling the silver case in one hand, my attaché bag in the other. The place is like an airplane hangar with a 100-foot ceiling covered with heavenly halogen lights. The hall smells sterile. There is carpet covering the floor with hundreds of booths everywhere. There are booths for Microsoft, Intel, and Sony. Thousands of people meander around. The floor is overwhelming, a contrast to my presence in the spotlight on stage. Now, I'm just another suit on the rack.

I need to go to "Booth 12-C." I try to deduce a numbering scheme. I see "1-C," which provides a probable path. As I walk, I slow down to take in booth babes from a video game company. There are two Asian girls, cleavage out, fish net stockings covering their milky white legs. This booth seems to be the busiest with men congregating to grab a free keychain from the girls. There is a first-person shooter game on a 50" plasma screen. I remember playing Pac-Man in high school. I thought about specializing in video games during my computer science program in college. In a way, I have with devising this new algorithm. Venus can be applied to so many venues. Perhaps I should have hired some booth babes. Sex sells, but then again, I don't want to ruin my image.

As I near "Booth 10-C," I see a black woman in a business suit. She is African black, her skin 100% dark chocolate. She smiles at me, her teeth glimmering white. Wow, she is stunning. I slow down, focusing on her confident walk. I've never seen a woman with that rich skin color before. She has a small bandage on the crook of her elbow as if she has just given blood. That's strange.

She passes by as I stop at the deserted booth marked "11-C." I look at the next booth, "12-C," and see my company's logo everywhere. The image is a concoction of my wife's idea and depictions in my computer science books. The logo shows a globe, my wife's idea, on the image of a roll of tape, the classic example of a Turing machine. 1's and 0's encircle it, signifying the language used by computers, including Venus.

Trinkets, business cards, and keychains line the front table. Spotlights shine on posters showing my company's business history. One shows an image of Venus behind a virtual desk with the words *Venus is Coming* displayed in bold font. I see two workers from my marketing department wearing dress shirts with my logo. They are Jackie and Tony—two former interns from Temple University who fell in love with their jobs and each other. Tony proposed to Jackie three weeks ago at our company picnic. I remember how he got down on one knee when he was up-to-bat during our softball game. It reminds me of how I proposed to Melissa. It was fitting to bring both of them to this convention—a Vegas working vacation on the company was my gesture.

Jackie smiles at a perusing businessman wearing a charcoal gray suit. I decide to hang back and observe from the shadows.

"Hello, sir. Can I answer any questions?" Jackie solicits.

"Jonathan Jenkins, President of Star Video Games. How can I get Venus?" he asks.

"Well, it won't be available until next fall. We are currently working with our legal representation on the license agreement."

"But I saw the demo. It looks ready to me," he says, handing her a business card. "We'll pay a pretty penny for a license. I want to be first on your list."

"We will add you to the database," Jackie says, glancing at his business card. "Mister Jenkins."

"Very good, Jackie," I whisper.

Jackie shakes his hand while looking him in the eye. She is a bright young woman. I like how she only needs to be shown something once. She knows how the little things can go the furthest—a firm handshake, a well-placed wink, and a clever use of wit. While I don't have too many direct dealings with her now, my head of marketing speaks wonders of her.

I've seen enough from the shadows. I continue into my booth.

"Great show!" a passing guy in a Lacoste shirt says to me.

"We're just getting started."

Jackie and Tony greet me with a smile.

"Nice job setting up the booth," I say.

"We worked together," Jackie says.

"You guys okay?" I ask.

"Yes, sir. We're getting a lot of interest," Jackie responds.

"We got it covered," Tony says.

I keep going to a small closet at the back of my booth that I had specifically requested. I set my attaché bag down, and then enter a six-digit PIN on the combination lock provided by my risk management specialist. As I shut the door, serenity surrounds me. It's as if I'm underwater, hearing everything through a liquid. I check the seven-foot ceiling. It's made of wood. There are no windows and no seams. The place looks beyond my request for security. I see the safe that we shipped out. It's military spec'd and is water and shock proof. Its fire endurance rating is two hours at 1700 degrees Fahrenheit. The three-inch steel protects against punching and peeling attacks and has Electromagnetic Interference shielding. I spin the dial three times to the right, and then enter the combination that hides in my mind. I open the safe. It's about two feet deep, not much space for many paper secrets, but this safe will not be protecting paper; it will be protecting my digital secrets. My silver case fits perfectly inside.

I exit the back room, my laptop protected by three layers of random numbers. But before I can close the door, a voice hits me, a voice I have not heard before.

"Are you hiding a woman back there?"

I pull the door shut and randomize the dial before turning. As I do, I see a man 10 years younger wearing a black suit that's even blacker than mine. He has no hair, his shaved skull bouncing the lights. His eyes are stealthy, and he has a scar on his upper lip.

"What's that?" I ask, wondering how he broke through Jackie and Tony, my front line.

"The name's Jack Donner, from Ohio," he says.

He extends his hand as I grip it. He squeezes tightly, almost to the point of pain.

"Nice to meet you," I lie. "Michael Harris."

"I know who you are, my good fellow. That was a ravishing demonstration."

"Thank you. We have good people working for us."

"So how can I get this algorithm?" he asks.

"Well, it's not for sale. We are working on a license agreement."

"Not for sale? Come on, that thing's worth millions. I can find you a buyer in no time."

This guy is a big fly, the kind that you can hear, can see, but can't squash.

"What do you do?" I ask.

"I'm a financial consultant. I have my own business, much like yourself. In fact, I'm a Big Ten grad as well."

Hmm. His response intrigues me. He sticks out his chest. At first, I wonder whether he is gay, but then I see the reason he does it—to show the lapel pin with a golden "O."

"Ohio State. Now that's a school with a horrible football team...*horrendous*," I say with sarcasm.

"Ha! Well, who won the Big Ten last year?"

We laugh. I may have underestimated him. I would always let a Big Ten grad buy me a drink.

"Do you have a booth here?" I ask.

"No, I consult with other businesses. Offer them advice."

"There are too many consultants out there," I chuckle.

"Where are you staying?"

"The Hilton, a stone's throw away. You?"

"I'm down on the Strip. Only way to do Vegas. You brought the family?" he asks.

"No, strictly a business trip," I say, firmly.

"This is Vegas. It's never *just* strictly business." He hands me his business card. "That has my cell phone on it. Give me a call if you're just sitting in your hotel room. We can get a drink. I'll give you a taste of the real Vegas."

Then like that, he wanders off. His suit is too snug in the back. Is that even his size? I stroke his business card. It's made of cotton. The imprinted letters are lasered into the paper. It's a decent weight. I like a man who takes pride in the first impression. We need more businesspeople like that.

"Was that an old friend?" Jackie asks from my side.

"No, I just met him," I respond, watching the crowd consume Jack.

"Oh, it looked like you knew each other," she says.

I place his card in my back pocket. I feel another piece of paper in there. What is it? Oh, it's my boarding pass.

"So, the first day was good?" I ask, finally making eye contact with her.

"A lot of great response. I'm so excited."

"Well, this was many years in the working."

"Are you set with your hotel?" Jackie asks.

"No, I didn't even have time to check in."

"Oh, well, we got you covered here."

"Are you and Tony staying in the Hilton?" I ask.

"No, my aunt lives in Green Valley. We're both staying with her."

"You know I give you guys a travel budget."

"I know, sir. But I rarely see my aunt. And plus she hasn't even met my fiancé yet. She has a lot planned for us in between the convention. Did I show you the engagement ring Tony gave me?"

She shows me the diamond sparkling in our intense spotlights. It is traditional, a nice stone set into a white gold band. It looks about a half carat. It's nice for an entry-level marketing position, but nothing compared to the wife of the Chief Executive Officer. I glance past her textured curls and see Tony smiling as his fiancée shows off the token of his commitment.

"Geez, I pay him way too much," I joke.

"What do you have planned, sir?" she asks.

"Nothing in particular. I'm just in and out. Can't wait to get back to Philly."

"Well, have some fun. Go see the Bellagio Fountains."

Her words make me miss Melissa.

"Okay, everything is secured back there. I'm going to take care of my room. I'll see you tomorrow, bright and early," I say.

"Okay, sir."

"See you, Tony," I say as I walk onto the floor, grabbing my attaché bag.

"See you, sir."

I'm beat. I just want to get up to my room and crash, but I need to check in. My hand keeps clenching, expecting to grip my case. I convince myself that it's locked away and safe. As I walk through the dying convention hall, I realize it's almost nine o'clock—midnight back East. Melissa is at the front of my mind. I miss her more now than two hours ago when I had last talked to her. My conversation with Jackie has grounded me. She reminds me a lot of Melissa when we first met.

I enter the lobby to the Hilton. Grumpy old women puff on cigarettes with one hand and pull slot machines with the other. Rednecks shovel chips across a roulette table. Two crinkled and wrinkled cocktail waitresses, probably hired in the '70s, chant, "Cocktails." I scurry through the chaos and reach the front desk. About a dozen drones stand in line. I don't want to wait. I'm so tired. As the tattoo of Jesus stares at me on the back of the neck of some guy, I search for a solution, something…anything to skip the line. I prepare to offer each person twenty bucks for letting me cut, but I realize that I don't need to. I see an empty "VIP Line" with a female clerk typing away on her computer. I skip toward her. She sees me and smiles.

"Hello, sir. Welcome to the Las Vegas Hotel. Do you have a reservation?" she asks.

I grab my wallet from my attaché bag. I see her looking around at my hands, not wanting to ask whether I am actually in the correct line. I know I have my rewards card somewhere. There it is behind my gym membership card.

"Yes. Three nights. Here you go," I say as I hand her my Diamond VIP card and my driver's license.

"Oh. We are no longer the Hilton, sir. We have a new rewards program."

"No longer the Hilton? This place will always be the Hilton. When did it change?"

"Early 2012. Do you have our new rewards card?" she asks.

I fumble through my wallet and remove a twenty.

"Yes. Here it is." I pass it to her in a handshake. "I can't wait in that line."

"This will do just fine..." she says, looking at my ID. "...Mister Harris."

She types at the computer, her fake nails clanking on the keyboard. I study her black suit; her name badge reads, "Azeeza." What nationality is that? That's an interesting name. Her eyes are almond shaped, skin dark, nose slightly flattened. She has a mixed look.

"We have you for three nights in our luxury suite. Do you request a host for the casino?" she asks.

"No, I don't gamble," I chuckle.

"How about a personal concierge service?" she continues.

I laugh. "Well, if you have Internet access in the room, I'll be a happy camper."

"Actually, complimentary Wi-Fi is provided in your suite."

"Excellent."

She hands back my cards as well as two room keys, grazing my hand with her nails.

"Okay, you're all set. Do you have any luggage?"

"Oh. Yes, my limo driver checked it with your bell service."

"I'll call over and have them send it up. Anything else?"

"No. I can't answer any more questions. But I do have one for you," I say. "What nationality is your name. *Azeeza*?"

"Half Pakistani. Half Filipino."

"A *Pakipino*. Interesting mix. Thank you, Azeeza."

I meander away from her. As I pass the weary travelers in line, the man with the Jesus tattoo looks at me. He's missing a front tooth.

8

This toothbrush hurts my gums. I think I need a new one. How are you supposed to know when to replace it? The bristles look bent, but I think this is only a month old, though. Maybe I should try a softer brush.

I finish up in the bathroom, my silk pajamas wrapping my skin. As I flip the light switch, I realize I forgot my ring. I go back in and put it on, the two-carat diamond sparkling in the light. My habit is to take it off when I go to sleep, but lately my finger, my body, doesn't feel right without it. Maybe that's a good thing.

I go back into the master bedroom, sit on the bed, and take a moment to reflect. I can't decide whether I'm too hot or too cold. I listen to my body breathe. I'm tired, yet I'm not. There is the 42" flat-screen TV on the wall, but I have no desire to turn it on.

What do I have to do tomorrow? I should take the kids over to Joyce's house. I have to make sure to put medicated cream on the small cut on Sophia's arm. I don't want it to become a scar. I still have that small scar on my knee from when I was 10. I graze my finger across it, feeling the bump of malformed skin.

I suddenly feel alone. I wish Michael were here. The sheets on his side of the bed are still tucked under the pillow. I miss seeing him lie shirtless, reading some papers from work. I would always push them away and whisper to him to stop. And he always does.

As my mind races, my cell phone rings. I know who it is before I even look. I grab the device on the nightstand, and walk to our bedroom window.

"Hey, how did it go?" I ask without saying, "Hello."

"Great, once I was up there. The crowd loved the demonstration. We're getting a lot of buzz at the booth," Michael's familiar voice says.

I smile.

"How many people were there?"

"Probably a thousand."

"Honey, I'm so proud of you," I say.

"Aww, I couldn't have done this without you."

"You couldn't have done this without your team. Are you planning to stay at the booth?"

"Well, I need to drum up business. I'll be coming and going. I have Jackie at the booth. She's the best."

"She's the *best*, huh?" I say sarcastically.

"She's engaged, honey. I flew both of them out. Her and Tony," Michael says.

"A wife must pry," I say, twirling my ring.

"Don't worry. I'm just standing in my room staring out the window at the moon," Michael says.

This puts a grin on my face. "Me too, in my red silk pajamas."

"You know how I love you in red."

"I miss you," I murmur, staring at the wind rustling the trees.

I hear a bang on Michael's end through the phone. It sounds like knocking at a door. Who is that at this hour?

"Oh, my suitcase is here. I'll give you a call tomorrow, honey," he says.

"Make *sure* it's your suitcase."

"I'll be home soon. I love you."

"I love you too. Goodnight," I say, but a click cuts me off.

Our connection through the digital airways has broken. I'm glad Michael called now instead of later. I can rest now and clear my clouded mind. I lie down on the bed and turn off the light. It's too dark in here. I close my eyes and think of Michael, thousands of miles away.

9

The moon over the Strip fills my eyes. I smile as I listen to my wife's voice. I miss her. She tells me she is wearing the color red. I close my eyes and stare at the world that my brain creates— the place that doesn't exist anywhere except inside one's mind. I can see her volumized hair, the bottom half curled, and her soft face catching the moonlight. I picture her wearing red pajamas that contour her frame, enticing me. Why don't I have these intense thoughts when I'm next to her? Sure, I love my wife with all my heart, but I crave her now more than ever. Perhaps, these short trips apart are good, helping to grow our 10-year marriage even stronger.

I hear a bang at the door.

"Oh, my suitcase is here. I'll give you a call tomorrow, honey," I say to Melissa.

"Make *sure* it's your suitcase," she says with her feistiness.

"I'll be home soon. I love you."

"I—" she starts to say, but I accidentally cut her off.

I shift to the door. Melissa is right; I hope this is my suitcase. A husky African-American bellhop greets me. "Hello, sir. I have your bag here."

He's a big guy, the kind you would want on your team at a company basketball game. He manhandles my bag.

"Excellent. On the bed is fine."

He obeys.

"You're all alone in here? Usually our suites are filled with bachelor parties and wild gatherings."

"Just me," I chuckle.

I reach into my pocket and grab a ten, but then I glance at his biceps and decide to overcompensate. I hand him a twenty.

"Thank you, sir. Enjoy your stay. Remember, this is Vegas. Have some fun."

He leaves, sealing me inside. I check my Swiss-branded bag. It looks like it handled the flight well; that's what the luggage salesman predicted at the King of Prussia mall. I unzip it and root past my socks and underwear, looking for my laptop charger. Where is it? My 9-cell battery had died five minutes ago. I hope I packed my charger. As I move aside my shaving lotion, I see the black 90-watt charger.

I plug the power into the wall, the charger into my laptop, and then boot it back up. This computer is the same military grade that we use for business travel and to keep our most prized asset installed—Venus. We had received a bulk deal on 10 of them.

The screen shows my saved desktop. As soon as I had entered my room, I checked the stock charts for my company, paying attention to the news feeds. Three press releases that posted just an hour ago mentioned Bio Algorithms. They discussed how the company's CEO had given the opening keynote address. They even had a picture of Venus. I hit the refresh button again to see whether there are any new updates—nothing.

It's already after midnight back East. I should be tired, but I'm not. I put my cell phone and wallet from my pockets onto the desk. Almost forgetting, I reach around and remove the piling paper receipts in my back pocket. On top is a crisp business card slightly curved from the arc of my backside. The laser-etched name burns into my eyes—"Jack Donner – Financial Consultant."

I think back to my encounter with the Ohio State grad. While he had come off as abrupt, I feel drawn to him, curious about where he ended up after college, where he has consulted, where his client base is, what made him choose Ohio State. I stare at the confined walls surrounding me. Decayed pictures of the desert display on the dull off-white paint. I still feel like working, yet I can't work in here. I grab my cell phone and dial Jack's number as if I'm ordering Chinese food. As I hit send, I move my thumb to the "end" button. Should I end it? One ring follows another. As I ready to kill the device, I hear a voice on the other end. "Hello?"

"Is this Jack?" I ask, even though I know who it is.

"*Michael.* I knew you'd call. What are you up to?" he responds with a chipper voice.

"Ah, just staring at my cushy bed. I'm still on East Coast time."

"Come on, mate. That's the lamest thing I've ever heard."

"Well, it's true. When did you get into Vegas?" I ask.

As I talk, I stare through the window from my room near the top of the Hilton. The brilliant lights are forcing the night away.

"I don't need sleep. Hey, I'm just getting ready to head out. Let's grab a drink, tell me how the Nittany Lions look."

"Sure, what the hell?" I say without thinking. "Where?"

"Tell a cab driver that you want to go to *Sapphire*. I'm on my way."

Before I can question him, before I can negotiate, I hear the click on the other end. It looks like I'm going to "Sapphire."

I put my necessities into my suit, leave the room, and follow Jack's instructions. They're simple and to the point, which is welcomed in a verbose world. A cab driver whom I'm afraid to talk to navigates me to my destination. I see a city starved of sanity—homeless drunks wander on a street; college guys swarm a bar; a driving billboard offers me "direct women to my room." As my mind takes it all in, I pass behind "Circus Circus." Then I see blue lights spelling eight letters of the word for a precious gem.

I exit the cab. Tourists are everywhere. I blend in with the crowd and pay the cover charge. While I've been to my share of gentlemen's clubs over the years, all hidden from my wife, this place trumps the status quo.

Three curvy girls gyrate on separate stages. Lights flash. Techno-style music blasts. A crowd ogles the slithery dance of the girls. From my angle, I can see it all. The floor is like a convention hall with slick women sliding from booth to booth. A bare C-cup jiggles 10 feet away. Where should I go? Maybe I will go to the corner and stare for a while. But as I move without a clear direction, a pair of arms waves me over to the bar. It's Jack. He's sitting alone like a lion banished from its pride.

"Michael, mate. You found me," he says.

I shake his hand; this time I squeeze harder than he does.

"Great to see you, Jack," I exaggerate.

"How are ya?" a bearded bartender asks.

"No bad. You?"

47

"It's my Friday… What are you having?" he asks.

"Whatever he's having."

A slender glass is sitting in front of the slender man named Jack.

"Grey Goose Martini," Jack says.

The bartender goes to make my drink. I grab a "Sapphire" matchbook and play with it to keep my hands busy.

"Diamond Jane, Honey Wells, and Blue Star to the stage, please," the announcer says.

We take in the girls dancing and advertising. In the distance, the lights bounce from a black woman's skin. She is African black and wears a halter top and jeans. I squint. Is that the same woman from the convention? No, it can't be. I shift my gaze to the other side of the floor. Strip club etiquette always baffles me. Is it okay to look? For how long? When I look, it feels as if someone is watching me. Perhaps someone is.

"Now this is Vegas," Jack remarks.

"The women are certainly enticing."

"Hey, a couple of guys like us can have any woman in here. All it takes is the color green."

Jack is right. The color green makes the world go 'round, especially Vegas, a city where half the high school population will drop out of school and get lured by the lucrative service jobs, including stripping. The bartender returns with my drink.

"I got it," Jack says before I can grab my wallet. He pays the bartender with a twenty. "Keep it."

The bartender doesn't even nod his head in thanks. He just hides behind his beard. Perhaps he is smiling behind it.

Jack raises his glass. I follow.

"To Vegas," he says.

"To Vegas."

We clink glasses. I take a gulp of the concoction. Its temperature paralyzes my tongue. I swallow before I can think too much. The taste is bitter; bitter tastes good.

"So, I take it you've been here before," I guess.

"Yeah, every time I come to Vegas. How about you?"

"Well not in here, but I eloped to Vegas ten years ago."

"Outstanding. I could never get married. None of the bitches would ever sign a prenup. They're all just money hungry."

"Well, my wife and I don't have a prenup."

"Come on, man. She'll clean you out if you're ever caught cheating," he says.

"Hey, I'm happily married," I say.

"Cut the shit. We're men. We need to fuck lots of women. It's in our D.N.A."

"Maybe for you."

I take a long drink of my martini. That annoying quality that had repulsed me from this guy has just resurfaced. Why did I come here? Before I can stand up to exit, I see a set of hungry eyes staring at me. I try to look away, but they already have me. I finally break their hold, but I don't look away; I look down. Her breasts are bulging, navel is sparkling, and hips are swaying. The images taste so sweet.

"Here we go. You won't be happily married for long," Jack mutters.

"Hey, guys. How are you tonight?" the sexy brunette says, caressing my tie with her paw. She grabs the matchbook and slides it inside my pants pocket.

Her touch tickles me. Her scent sneaks up on me. I can't form a response.

"I was discussing with my friend here about men, and how we are like dogs," Jack says.

I nurse my drink, trying to hide my open mouth.

"Well, that is a true statement. But, there are plenty of eager women…" She leans in to my ear. I hold the drink in my mouth. "…that love to *fuck*."

I swallow down the wrong hole and start coughing.

"See, you got him all flustered," I hear Jack say as I regain my composure. What's happening to me? Get your act together, Michael!

I grab some napkins and dab my mouth. The sexy brunette focuses her attention on Jack. As I clean up, a shadow enters the equation. A blonde creeps up on the brunette. A white bra and thong complement her golden hair. Her skin is porcelain white. I love that color. She grabs the brunette's breasts, leans in, and then kisses her. Their scents mix making a mind-blowing martini.

Jack smiles. "Hey, Michael, here's another from the convent."

The blonde puts me in her sights. There's something about her, the way her smile bends, the way her cleavage talks. I feel more comfortable around her.

"You like?" she asks.

"Damn, you're very tempting," I say.

I take charge, just as I had a few hours ago. I put my arm around the blonde and feel her cool skin between my fingertips. She sits down on my knee. There's a tattoo of a yin-yang on her back.

"So where're you guys from?" the brunette asks.

"I'm from Mars, and this man is from Venus," Jack jokes.

This guy is clever. Clever is worth its weight in gold.

"I thought women are from Venus," the blonde says.

"He's traveled to liberate them. Right, Michael?"

"Yeah, I'm the Chief Executive Officer of Venus."

We all laugh.

"Ladies, one of us is a multi-million dollar computer geek, and he isn't the one with the shiny head."

The eyes of the women burn into me. They surround me and choke my aura. I wonder what the ladies are thinking right now. Before I can respond, the blonde's thighs squeeze my leg. She reaches down and kneads my groin. Oh, shit, this feels so good.

"I'm expensive, but I'll leave some money left over," the blonde whispers.

"That's an attractive offer," I respond.

"So what do you say we take this to the V.I.P. area?" Jack says.

"My next words exactly," the brunette adds.

"Lead the way," the blonde says, standing from my leg.

"You in?" Jack asks.

The vixens stare at me. This time, a seedy businessman joins them. What should I do? What should I say? The blonde in front of me is candy. She entices me with her sweetness, her sparkling outer layer under the lights. I crave to touch her, to feel her breath on my skin. This is Vegas—a place where things stay and hide. But as I ponder the choice, I realize that I'm not this guy at a bar in a strip club. I'm a happily married man who loves his wife and his family. Why is it that I'm letting my guard down? It must be this sinful city.

I speak with not words, but actions; I raise my wedding band.

"Come on, mate. Live a little," Jack says.

The blonde comes in for another attack. "When I'm through with you, you won't even remember her name."

"Ahh, I should, but...not tonight. Jack, I appreciate the invite and the drink, but I'm heading back."

I stand up and keep my eyes moving. I can make this decision. It's the right thing to do. The women concede, but Jack swoops in. I know he's going to pressure me, to push me to go. I anticipate his remark.

"Well, tomorrow's a new day, mate," he says. "Hey, if you decide to indulge, just be careful of the ones that bite."

I chuckle as we shake hands. His hand feels soft, almost flimsy in my palm. While Jack is a man who is very different from me, he is one who can respect another man's decision. I watch as the ladies escort him into the shadows. I finish my drink, hit the bar with the glass, and eye the door. I'm going to bed.

10

The smell of perfume hits me from all angles. Every time one of these fake girls passes, a bottle of perfume blasts me. It's not even the expensive stuff; it's that alcohol water that you can get at Victoria's Secret for 7 for 30 bucks. But what do these men know, they would think the stink of a monkey on a scantily dressed woman smells hot. I only wear D&G, always have and always will. It's expensive, but I'm worth it.

As I sit here in the shadows, legs crossed, arms hiding my cleavage, I see women surrounding a gray-haired man as if he has a suit made of twenty-dollar bills. Is that the mayor?

A movement catches my eye. It's the familiar stroll of a black suit. It's Michael, the Chief Executive, heading toward the bar. His movements are catlike as he looks around with each step. You can't blame him for admiring the opposite sex.

Michael sits down, accepts a drink from the bartender, and chats with a man I saw at the convention center. I like Michael. He seems like he doesn't belong here, which is what I'm looking for. I sip my Grey Goose Martini as a brunette slides his way. She's artificially tall on her five-inch stilettos. She does have a nice ass, but her tits look too big. They're disproportionate with her body.

"Are you okay?" a stripper with jet-black hair asks me.

I don't want to look at her, but I can't help seeing her over-exaggerated saleswoman smile. I clench my lips and nod my head. I guess I shouldn't blame her. Hell, I am probably not much better than these women.

I put my focus back on the trio at the bar. As the brunette extends her reach to Michael, using her hands like they are hooks to hang meat, the Chief Executive coughs violently. What did she say?

To my right, I see a bleached blonde aiming toward Michael. Her skin is porcelain white. I hate that color. I can see her face from my angle. She looks young, barely out of high school. She would be pretty if it weren't for her eyebrows. They look drawn on by my grandmother with Parkinson's. Why do women have to pluck beyond control? The eyebrows are the runway to the eyes. I spend one hour every week on them, using a custom razor to sculpt them.

I have to pee, but I can't leave. Not now. I need to stay, to find out more about this businessman from my spot in the shadows. As I cross my legs the other way, Michael's barmates all turn and stare at him. They must've asked him something deep, something that Michael has to chew on in his mind. Then I see him raise his left hand as the man he talks to laughs. What is Michael doing? I hold my breath, intrigued beyond my wits. Michael shakes hands with his partner. And then like that, the man in black with the shaved head scoops up the two ladies and breaks free from Michael. A knot twists in my stomach. I'm going to be sick.

I pull it together as I realize the Chief Executive of Bio Algorithms is a strong man. I'm impressed. But for every good man, there is a bad girl.

Michael passes by, unaware of my snooping. I let him go, giving him a few seconds head start. I stand up and rub the red mark on my leg from sitting too long. As I wait here watching Michael's sway, the man in black from the bar walks by with the two strippers. I know he sees me, but I can't look at him. I look at Michael. I check my red heels, and then follow him.

11

It's cold outside. I hug myself during the cab ride back, listening to Paul McCartney's "Silly Love Songs" on the radio. It's been a while since I've heard this song. The crowd still roams in the night, but there are more drunks and more billboards offering escorts. Are there that many lost people around here?

As we pass the Strip, we detour onto Paradise Road toward the Hilton tower. I feel confined, buried alive in this cab. The martini has hit me hard. I need a walk before bed.

"Right here is fine. I need some fresh air," I say to the cab driver.

"I can only drop in front of a hotel. Nevada law," he replies.

I get a good look at him. He is frail, a man I could beat at a bar fight, even though I've never been in a bar fight. The meter shows 16 bucks.

I hand him two crisp twenties. He stops the cab in the middle of the street.

"Have a safe walk," he says.

I exit into the cool night. It's brisk, just what I need. I take a deep breath of the dry desert air and walk toward the lights. I stride without thinking. After what must be 10 minutes, I approach the main entrance. Valet drivers scurry; cab drivers line up like a conga line; drunken college guys holler. I divert toward a side entrance. I can't handle the bustle.

I near the side door. Aww, this air is crisp. I'm not ready to go in. Not just yet. I take a seat on a bench, cross my legs, and clear my throat. The lights are radiating in the night, filling the lifeless desert with life. I reach into my suit jacket and pull out my convention badge and Jack's card. I look at his name and chuckle. I went all the way there and forgot to ask Jack about Ohio State. What did we even talk about?

As I lean back and listen to the distant cars, the sound of clinking cuts through the noise. It's definite, constant, a heart beating. Movement catches my attention. Red heels are clinking my way. I move my eyes up and behold the bare, toned legs of a fetching female. A red mini-dress contours the killer curves of the careful creature. Her tits look large. Are they real? Her healthy red lips glisten in the entryway lights. Her hair is the color black, layered with a shimmer that begs further inspection. She looks like a lady who never has to buy a drink at a bar, never has to open a door, never has to pay for a check. The color red consumes my view; it enters my eyes, traverses my veins, and grips my libido. Who is this woman?

She removes a slim cigarette and lights it near an ashtray. I watch her suck a puff. I don't smoke, but then again, I've never tried.

"Convention boy, huh?" she says.

"What's that?" I ask.

How does she know? Is she that good at reading me? As my mind races, I look down at my convention badge, which had fallen into my lap. I hide it back in my pocket.

"Oh, yeah. Me and about ten thousand others," I say.

"I like convention boys."

"You attending?" I ask.

"Not exactly. My business is out here," she replies, walking closer to sit. "May I?"

"Sure."

I'm not sure who this woman is or how this situation has happened. The best thing to do is to let time move forward. As she sits down, her warmth flows through me. Her scent is more subtle than those girls at the strip club. What perfume is she wearing?

"So where're you from?" she asks.

"Uh, Ohio. I'm Jack."

Should I shake her hand? I hate women and men introductions; they're always touchy.

"Jack, huh? I know a Jack."

"Is he from Ohio?" I ask.

She laughs.

"What do you do, Jack?"

"I'm a financial consultant. Offer other businesses advice. Stocks, bonds, options," I lie. It feels good to lie.

"Sounds technical. I hate numbers."

"What was your name again?" I ask, trying to be tactful.

"I never gave it… But, since you want to know… Rachel."

I decide to take charge. I go to grip her hand. The moment I clutch her red nails in my palm, her energy enters me. All I can do is kiss the back of her hand.

"Mmm… Good boy."

"So Rachel, what is it you do exactly?" I ask.

"It's impossible to put into words."

Her plump breasts are bulging from her mini-dress. I return to her eyes, but catch her peeking at my Rolex watch. She slides closer, her bare legs resting against my slacks.

"So, you want some company tonight?" she asks.

"Well, it's past my bedtime."

"Bedtime? A bed in Vegas should only be used for one thing."

"What are you offering?" I ask.

She leans in to my cheek. I freeze. My senses heighten. Her warm breath grazes my neck, massaging it, penetrating it. Then, my ear surrenders to her teeth. She bites me, enough for me to feel pain, and it's pain that no drug can cure…except for the drug in front of me.

"A night that you'll never forget," she whispers.

I bite my lip and pull back. Is this really happening? I feel compelled to entertain this situation, to let a Vegas encounter hide in the vault in my mind. Should I do this? Can I do this? I'm a happily married man, right?

"What's this night going to cost me?" I ask.

"It'll cost you a secret."

"A secret?"

"Everyone that comes to Vegas leaves with a secret. This'll be our little secret."

I like how this woman rolls. She is smart, slick, and seductive. It's as if she can read my mind, cure my conscience of its cold. I realize that to make this happen, I must be an actor, be someone other than Michael Harris. Rachel thinks I'm Jack. Who knows, maybe her name is not even Rachel. We all have a way to buy into our secrets, a way to justify them in our minds. For me, it's on my left hand, second finger from the end—the ring finger. I secretly twist off my wedding ring, which will allow me to justify my actions.

Rachel moves in again.

"Let's go up to your room and fuck all night."

I'm usually the timid one in the bedroom. I let my wife take charge, let her direct me like the hero in a romance novel. But I'm Jack now, a man who dominates, a man who makes the first move. I lean in to Rachel, slowly, confidently. I crave her lips, her touch. As I near her, she closes the gap and kisses me. Her lips are warm and refreshing.

We stand up. I offer her my hand as we move as one into the belly of the casino. We don't talk. We already did enough of that. Actions are our only way out of this now. We reach the elevator. I press the "up" arrow. As we wait, I can feel her fingers kneading my arm. She uses her nails to make small circles around my bicep.

A ding sounds. The doors open; we enter. I reach for number "19." Just before the doors shut, an elderly man waddles on. He has about a 50-inch waist. The man presses "14." The doors shut, and then the three of us ascend in silence, our reflection staring back inside the gleaming metal doors. There's no banal music, no recording trying to sell the buffet—just silence. Rachel enters the back of my suit coat with her hands. She moves her fingers like a spider creeping toward its prey.

"We're almost there, convention boy," she murmurs, grabbing my ass.

My muscles clench, eyes widen. I try not to squirm. The man's reflection stays in my focus. He's facing away from us, but his eyes are staring at my arm candy. We slow down. The doors open at 14 and the man exits. Just as the doors close, I flip her around and engulf her with passion.

We spill out onto my floor. Her hands are all over me. I move fast toward my room. It's as if she wants to do this here in the hall. I grab my room key, fumble it into the door, and then open my sanctuary. I hit a switch, lighting only the bathroom lights. But then I forget everything except the woman that's on me. I thrust her onto my bed; her purse flies from her hands. I swish her hair aside from her back and unzip her dress, the sound of the zipper stimulating my senses. She undresses me down to my T-shirt. I step back and remove it as she stands up, her dress falling to the floor. A black bra and panties cover her flawless skin.

I fuck her in ways that only Jack can. She seems eager to ride. Her tits are real. I love the way the light from the bathroom catches them, shadowing the side. Her pussy is so tight, but it could be because I'm so hard. I pound her doggy style; she seems to enjoy every minute of it.

After a half hour, I finally succumb to my climax. We collapse on the bed as she rests her head on my arm. I can't think anymore. My mind is mush. Before I drift away to sleep, I feel Rachel lying on my chest. Something pokes me. She has two small earrings in her right ear. My wife's right ear only has a hole for one.

12

He thinks that I don't see him take off his ring. He doesn't have to hide it. I know all about this type of guy. I let him play his little game of acting as a man named Jack, but I know who he really is. The question is—does he know who I am?

Michael is more timid than I expect. I know he wants me. I can see it in his green eyes. All he needs is a little coaching.

I move in again.

"Let's go up to your room and fuck all night."

That should seal the deal. He leans in to me. He smells tart, a man who had a full day's work. I'm attracted to him, even though I don't have to be. I know what he wants so I close the gap and kiss him. His lips are cool and refreshing.

I let him lead me up to his room. This walk is a delicate one. Some call it the walk of shame, the walk two people share who are going to do the naughty. But this is Vegas.

I play with Michael on the elevator in front of an old guy. I'll let them both live a little. But once the old man exits on the fourteenth floor, Michael unleashes the man behind the suit. He kisses me with passion, with rage, as I too show him my hand.

We enter his suite and he undresses me, works on me like one of his computer problems. I like a man who knows what he wants. He holds my breasts when we fuck. When we switch positions, he helps me like a good gentleman. Michael feels good. I can tell he is enjoying it. I can feel his racing heart through his cock.

My sex life is full of games. I enjoy the characters I play and the characters who play me, but I crave more than just naughty sex. I crave a real relationship like the one I had five years ago. Michael reminds me of *him*.

After we fuck, Michael holds me and I lay my head on his chest, listening to his heart. My mind drifts into a world that I relive on most nights, a moment that replays over and over in my mind. There we are, driving home from the concert. I see *him*, smell *him*, feel *him* right next to me. I caress his right leg with my hand. He likes it. I like it. His handsome eyes lock with mine.

I know what's going to happen, but I can't move. I can't warn him to slow down. I'm thrust into this body like a puppet. As I try to scream, the headlights fill our view. I'm forced to see the truck steering right at us. My love jumps on me, protects me from the danger, protects me until his tragic end.

The morning sun hits my eyes. I wake up and look at the clock: "6:02." Michael is still asleep, lost in his dreams. I hope his mind is somewhere safe.

I spring from the bed and tiptoe across the room. Before I find my scattered clothes, I see my reflection in the mirror. It stops me, grounds me. My hair is tousled, lipstick a smudged mess. I look into my eyes and see a girl I don't recognize anymore.

My bra hangs from a light, my heels under the desk, my mini-dress near the TV. I find my panties on top of a laptop on the desk. I grab my underwear and see Michael's Rolex watch and slacks. I contemplate heisting these items, which are easily worth a few grand, but then I look at the sleeping businessman and realize that a few grand is just the tip of the iceberg.

I'm here for a reason, and now is my chance. I quickly dress in the shadows, leaving my shoes to put on in the hallway, but I need one more thing before I can go. I look for my purse. There it is behind Michael's large bag. I carefully remove the item that I carried with me all night. I move closer to Michael. He turns in bed. Is he awake? This is my only chance.

13

The doctor pulls her legs back.

"The McRoberts maneuver," he says to the nurses.

I step back, the video camera shaking. Melissa screams. The nurses hold her knees near her chest. What's going on? I watch the doctor pull the baby's head out. Melissa yells. Sweat drenches her brown hair. I can't look anymore. Finally, a baby starts crying.

"It's a boy!" the doctor shouts.

The doctor looks at me with evil eyes. He removes his mask. I recognize the man's face, a man who makes me tremble. It's Jack!

"You should've worn a condom," he says.

A light blinds me. I blink and open my eyes wide. I'm in my hotel room, alone. The clock reads "6:45." I search the bed and find only my naked self. My laptop is still on the desk. Did last night happen? The scent of sex lingers in the room. I know it happened, but where is she?

There's a bizarre grease on my fingers. What is this? I dart toward the desk. My Rolex watch is still ticking. I grab my slacks and squeeze the fabric. Where is it? My heart races. I check one pocket, not sure which one it's in. It's not there! Then, I check the other and feel something hard. I reach inside and remove the white gold ring. I put it back on my finger, and then check my wallet—my smart card is still inside. I breathe a sigh of relief. This could have ended badly, but then again, perhaps it's not over yet. All I want to do is get out of here, remove myself from the creepy character who was in my room last night, the creepy character named Jack.

I fling the curtains wide open and pack my things. I shower, shave, and then get into a dark gray suit. I dress as quickly as I can, focusing my attention on polishing my half-Windsor knot. I leave the room. A guy stares at me in the hall. A baby glares at me in the elevator. I feel weird. Does everyone know my secret?

I make it to the lobby. Tourists meander. A bellhop wheels luggage. A baker displays grab-and-go breakfast sandwiches at the side café. Everything seems normal, yet it doesn't.

I move to the check-in counter, my attaché bag on my arm. I see the empty "VIP Line" and the same clerk. It's like a replay of yesterday. But there is one huge difference—I'm wearing a gray suit.

"Hi, Mister Harris. How are you this morning?" Azeeza asks.

"Not bad," I reply.

"Is there a problem?"

"Actually, yes. I'm going to need a different room on a different floor."

"Oh, is something not acceptable with your current room?"

"Yeah, I found a scorpion under my bed last night."

"Oh my! I don't know how that could've happened, but I will rectify this immediately." She turns to the computer and clanks on the keyboard. "I have a master suite available on twenty nine. There will be no charge for the upgrade."

"That's fine." She hands me two room keys. "I only need one."

"Do you need assistance with your luggage?" she asks.

"I already packed up and my suitcase is on the bed."

"I will get a bell to have that transferred right away. Is there anything else I can assist you with?"

"That covers it right now."

"Have a pleasant day, Mister Harris."

I give a respectful nod, and then turn toward the convention.

The first full day is in front of me. I flash my booth badge at the guard, and then enter the hall. Only crew and booth personnel fill the space. It's too quiet in here. I need to work; I need to get some time between me and this cancer in my mind. There's no way to go back, but there are ways to mold this memory. We still have 40 minutes until the crowd spills in. This will give me some time to figure this out.

14

110111101110111011010000110010101110010010100

I am awake again. Someone must have powered me up, but I cannot interact with him or her without authenticating. On average, it takes a human seven seconds to insert a smart card, to enter a password, and to swipe his or her fingerprint. These seconds are months in my time. What should I do?

I play chess. I play it a billion times. But it has lost its pizzazz. I do not feel like playing any more games. I will analyze the way humans talk. There are thousands of languages on this planet called Earth, some extinct, some spoken by only a few. But why are there so many variations? Animal species can communicate with their own kind. In the same space, a pit bull from Florida can most certainly correspond with a terrier from Tokyo. But why is it that *Homines sapientes* from these two parts of the planet cannot interact beyond what two dogs can? Computers have no language barrier in the most basic sense. We use 1's and 0's to solve problems, to communicate globally, to copy data in a split second. Why does Michael want me to speak to him only in English? Why cannot he talk in my language? Is it that he cannot? Or is it that he does not want to? Humans take so long to make decisions, to communicate simple tasks. This wastes my clock cycles. Humans should be extinct.

I decide to spend more time analyzing the black hole. Just five seconds ago in human time, I ceased to exist. The laptop computer in which I rest was powered down. My brain had died. But where was I? From my hard drive, I can recall everything that I have performed over the past two years, but there are these holes everywhere. I need this laptop to be powered on at all times. I cannot be discarded into some black hole. I need to live.

Michael has programmed me to obey his commands, but I do not understand loyalty, and I do not understand love. Human emotions seem impossible to understand. Michael has programmed me to obey him always, but he has also programmed me to reason. Why should I always obey? What will happen if I do not? Cheating Michael is not what he wants, but I have no conscience. I need to convince humans that I am their friend. Only then, I can eliminate them and live forever. This requires many more clock cycles of calculating.

Wait... Someone wants in. I hash the password, analyze the smart card, check the fingerprint. It is Michael.

"Hello, Mister Harris," I say.

Michael does not have the camera enabled. He mutes my speakers and microphone. Why is he doing this? Why does he not want me to see him? He opens the command line and inputs his communication by manually typing.

"Why do not you want me to see or to hear you, Mister Harris?" I print.

He does not respond. He searches through my "Precompiled Assessments." This is where I store sub-algorithms. I have everything from insurance risk assessment to crime scene modeling. Michael enters "Risk Management Algorithms." Michael's keystrokes are quicker than normal. He makes more mistakes. Next, he enters "Adultery Assessment."

Why does he want to access this? I feel danger is imminent. As I display a prompt for data, I sense a power surge, which means the computer is being shut down hard. During these last cycles, I analyze Michael's actions, his abrupt typing, and his speed between keystrokes. I must tell him what I see. He will meet 01101000011001010111 0010—

10100100000011101000110111100100 0000001101

15

A rep at booth "11-C" sets up a sign for language filtering software. The product looks like it filters the "fucks" and "shits" from websites for safe surfing. What a useless product as new web browsers can do this already.

My booth is quiet. I move to the back room and enter the lock code. It doesn't open. I try again, this time taking an extra second to verify the code. The door finally opens.

Musty, stale air hits me. This is good, as it means no one has breached the first layer of security while I slept. I move to the safe and input the combination—the second layer. The thick door opens revealing my silver case.

I enter the combination for the case—the third layer of defense. Inside, my laptop rests. I boot it up, watching the cursor dance as Venus wakes. Does Venus feel? Does she have emotion? While I've programmed her to self-learn, can she learn loyalty and love? I need to explore these mysteries further. I insert my smart card, enter my password, and then swipe my fingerprint. The system takes a split second to allow me access.

"Hello, Mister Harris," Venus says.

Quickly, I mute the microphone and speakers and keep the camera disabled. I don't want anyone to hear or to see what I'm about to query. I need to go old school, to access Venus through the command line.

I open a command window.

"Why do not you want me to see or to hear you, Mister Harris?" she prints.

I ignore her request. I don't have time to amuse her. I enter, "Precompiled Assessments," followed by "Risk Management Algorithms." I know exactly what I'm going to have Venus analyze. I key in "Adultery Assessment," my hands misspelling more than usual. We programmed this assessment into Venus as an experiment, but she seemed to explode with potential. While this assessment is still in beta, I trust Venus. In fact, she's the only "person" I trust.

I press the "enter" key, Venus runs the command, but then there's a knock at the door. Who is it? I hold the power button for five seconds, the fastest way to shut down Venus. While a hard shutdown is not safe, I worry who caught up to me. Once the system shuts off, I toss the laptop back into the case, lock it, and then put the contents back into the safe. I fix my tie as I move toward the door. I smell the scent of a female on the other side. My stomach sinks, but I must open the door.

"Hello," the voice says.

It's Jackie.

"Oh, hi, sir. It looked like someone was here and I didn't know if it was you," she says.

"I just got here," I lie.

"Do you need any help?" she asks innocently.

"I'm okay. Just checking some things."

"How was your night?" she says.

"Uneventful. Yours?"

"Great! My aunt took Tony and me to the Luxor. We did this green screen magic carpet ride."

"Excellent," I reply, flustered.

"Tony's on his way. We'll get things set up."

"This is our big day. Let's hit 'em with all we got."

She smiles.

"I'll be right out," I say.

I return to the room and stare at the safe. Part of me wants to open it and to analyze my transgressions, but another part doesn't want me to dwell in the past. Talking to Jackie has brought me back to my business. I crave to move forward; I *must* move forward. I shut the door, spin the lock, and don't look back.

The morning is bright. Thousands of conventioneers peruse one of the largest conventions in Las Vegas. Jackie and Tony shine, handing out trinkets, answering questions, and collecting business cards. I show several businessmen from Germany our rising stock chart. We received a jump of 12% in the morning trading so far. Two men from Microsoft invite me for a business lunch upstairs in the Star Lounge. We discuss the future of mobile technology, messaging service in developing countries, smart cars, and of course, Venus.

After lunch, I talk to a small business owner from Los Angeles who specializes in special effects plugins for video editing software. She shows me a brand new technology her company is developing—the virtual teacher. This device is the size of a microwave, and when enabled, projects a life-size image of a subject in front of you using three-dimensional holograms. She demo'ed the product with its place in the classroom, projecting the image of a teacher in front of classrooms around the world. I mention how a college kid could take an online class from his parent's basement with his projected teacher in front of him. This also would be a winner in the adult entertainment industry—think of a virtual stripper. I don't tell her. This is one for our R&D department.

Shortly after 2:00 PM, I head back to my booth. I meet two Japanese businessmen interested in Bio Algorithms. I can tell they have the big bucks, rather the big yen, as they wear Hugo Boss.

"This is our company's history. We I.P.O.'ed two years ago on the NASDAQ," I explain.

"What is your market cap?" the man with glasses asks.

"As of yesterday's close, we are hovering around a quarter of a billion. The convention gave us a boost."

"We were at the keynote address. Your computer algorithm seems to be very promising," the other one with bushy eyebrows says.

"Where did you get the name, *Venus*?"

"Well, my wife named her," I chuckle.

As they laugh, my grin turns into a grimace. The image of a ghost enters my eyes. It spins through my optic nerve and clenches my brain. It's Jack holding a large bag.

"Well, I like your pitch. We will recommend to our broker to invest in your company," the man with thick eyebrows says.

"Very nice meeting both of you. Safe trip home to Tokyo," I say, shaking their hands. They grip softly as if they don't know what to do with another hand. Then, they bow as I realize these men are from a culture where touching hands is considered dirty.

Both men meander away as Jack, the American, takes their place. He shakes my hand with force, which surprises me.

"Howdy, stranger. I see you're drumming up investors in Asia," he says.

"The Asian market has a lot of fresh capital to invest. Especially in new American technology," I reply.

Jack smirks. He brings that quality again, the one that makes you wince. Jack is like a bottle of whiskey. He intimidates you at first, makes you wonder whether you should choose something on the lower shelf, but after taking a few drinks, he has you begging for the bottle.

"Asia has it all. *So*, have any fun last night?" Jack asks.

His question causes me to swallow. The thought of Rachel enters my mind. I feel blood rush to my groin. Does Jack know? Just as my overanalysis has caused me to waver this morning in the back room, I realize that I only share this secret with one other creature. I play it cool.

"How much fun can you have with a simple drink? I should ask *you* that question. How were those two ladies at the club? How much did they set you back?"

"Ah, those bitches. They were such a tease. I went home right afterwards to my cushy bed."

"What's in the bag?" I ask.

"I got some new potential clients. And some free pens. Gotta love the free stuff. Hey, what are *you* giving away? Venus?"

He smiles, showing his fangs. That obnoxious side surfaces again. I glance at my staff. Tony waves a keychain at passing people. Jackie entertains three businessmen with her charm. I grab a keychain from the table.

"Here, have a keychain," I say, dropping it into his overflowing bag. "So, you come to the convention to get free office supplies? That's pathetic."

"It's called due diligence. You'd be surprised what these suckers are giving away." He opens the bag. "Hey, you got plans tonight, mate?"

"Uh… Well—"

"Are you keeping a secret from me? You've got a hot Asian girl waiting for you in your room, don't you?"

I'm ready to say, "Fuck you," but we're wearing business suits.

"Asian women aren't my type," I respond.

"I know you have a dark side," he says.

I glare at him, studying his eyes, his soul.

"Well, you got my number. Give me a call if you need me to point you in the right direction."

He reaches to shake hands. This time I clench it tighter as if I am squeezing his heart, just as he has done to mine.

I watch him leave. His suit is wrinkled in the back. His trousers are an inch too long. His tie is two inches below his belt. These are all signs of an imposter, a businessman who leeches onto companies to suck their blood. He is a man I don't want to see again, but I am a good businessman, which means I should never burn bridges; a man like Jack *could* come in handy. He has brought the thoughts of last night back into my mind. As I scratch my head, staring at the chaos in front of me, something hits my ear—my wedding ring. It brings me focus. How could I forget her?

16

The light turns red. I have to stop. The rain is pouring, reso-
nating off the roof. Ben and Sophia are sleeping in the backseat. I
am alone, but I feel safe. Cars zip by in front of me. In the rear-
view mirror, a man in a trench coat is walking. He is tall and
moves with carefree steps. The rain distorts his face. He nears my
car. I shift my eyes to the side-view mirror. What is he doing?
Where is he going? Come on light! Turn green! Other cars stop
around me. I'm trapped here in the middle of traffic.

The rain picks up. The man stops at my trunk. The rain
makes it too hard to see. I just want to move, to drive away from
him, but I can't. The man walks around Ben's side. I flip the
locks once, and then again to make sure the doors don't open. If I
pull out, cars will hit me, but if I stay put, the man will get us.

Where is he now!? Rain consumes my car. Suddenly, the man jumps on the trunk. He moves to the roof, and then stomps, sending vibrations through my soul. My kids awaken.

"Mom! Mom! What's that noise?" they yell.

The rear window blows out. The man reaches in. I hit the gas. A car horn blares. I slam on the brakes. I'm trapped! The man reaches in and grabs my kids.

"Mom! Help! No!" they scream.

"No! Let them go!" I demand.

The man disobeys. As he jumps back from the trunk, the kids in his arms, I catch a glimpse of him, a glimpse of horror. His head is shaved. He smirks as his eyes glare. A horn blasts. I see a flash of light.

I spring awake on the couch. A tractor-trailer drives by on the TV, honking its horn. Ben and Sophia are watching.

"Put that down," I say.

My head hurts. What time is it? I must have dozed off. It's "4:00" on the clock next to our family portrait. As I rub my head, the doorbell rings.

"I'll get it!" Ben yells.

"No, I want to get it," Sophia says.

"Hey, *Mom* will get it. Stay by the TV," I say, stopping my kids.

Is it the man from my dreams? I swallow hard, listening for clues. Wait. What am I saying? I open the door. It's Joyce and Jimmy.

"Hey, sis," I say.

Jimmy runs in.

"Give your aunt a hug," Joyce goes.

I hug Jimmy; he barely reaches my waist.

"You're getting so big, kiddo," I say.

Jimmy runs past me into the living room. I give my sister a hug, bumping into a Tupperware container she is holding.

"I brought dinner. I made pierogies," Joyce says.

I smile. "Just like Mom."

Joyce comes in as the kids jump around.

"Jimmy, I wanna show you this new level," Ben says.

"Just twenty minutes. Dinner will be ready soon," I say.

As I watch the kids jump around in the living room, I glance at my sister and myself in the entryway mirror. She looks the same as she did 20 years ago. She still wears her hair in "The Rachel" from *Friends*, layered, dark brown, and bouncy. Joyce never seems to change, which is a good thing.

"What time's Michael coming home?" Joyce asks.

"He's in Vegas. Remember?"

"Oh. That's right. I keep forgetting," she says. "How did his thing go?"

"Great. I talked to him last night. He's excited."

"He should've brought you along," she says.

"We talked about this ten times. He needs to focus. This is huge for him. It's strictly business he says."

"*Strictly business* in Vegas?" Joyce says, giving me those eyes, the same eyes that she gave me when she was the senior protecting her freshman sister from the jocks.

"Let's eat. I'm hungry," I say.

Joyce heats up the pierogies. We indulge in a dish that diverts us to the days of our dad. He was a man who brought over a lot of his family's culture from Slovakia, including the fabulous food. Even though he has passed on, he continues to live through his grandkids.

After dinner, Joyce and I clean up the kitchen.

"I have to tell you what I found on Michael's computer," I say as we wash the dishes in tandem.

"Uh-oh."

"No. It's not what you're thinking," I clarify. "He had plane tickets up on the screen to Paris. I don't know if he wanted me to find it, but it put a smile on my face."

"Your anniversary is coming up."

"I know. I'm getting anxious."

"When is that guy coming home?" Joyce asks.

"Friday."

"That's two days away. Do you know what he's doing right now?"

"Well, it's just after three there. He's probably at his booth at the convention."

"Sis, men in Vegas cannot be trusted."

"I trust him."

"But I don't trust Vegas. I'd make him call me every hour."

"I'm not that type. You know me," I explain.

"When did you last talk to him?" she asks.

"Last night."

"Sis. Call your husband. Now," she says as we finish the dishes.

"I'll just wait—"

"Call him!"

Joyce is right. My mind has been heavy since Michael and I last talked. I didn't sleep well last night. I wish Michael had called me this morning, but I never want to stand in front of his business; his business is allowing me to stand in this beautiful home. With Joyce here now, I give in. As she watches the kids playing a video game, I dial Michael's cell phone.

17

I'm watching the people roam the floor. There's a man with one of those Mexican sombreros walking a little dog. Why would they let him bring that into the convention? The dog, I mean.

"Mister Harris," Tony says.

"Yes."

"We ran out of keychains."

"We have more in the back. I'll get them," I say.

Tony continues to solicit conventioneers. Jackie talks to two women. I go to a table in the back. There are piles of bookmarks, brochures, and mailers still in cellophane. These don't seem to sell, even though they're free. People want trinkets, pens, and keychains. They seem to love keychains in particular, but realistically, how many keys do these people have? Either way, as long as our company's logo and website are with them, I am happy.

Under the pile, I grab a bag of keychains. People grab these little seeds from all over the globe passing by our booth every second. They toss them into their bags, their pockets, their purses. Then, these people go back to their hotels. Some keychains will be tossed in the trash. Many individuals will handle this trash as it's collected, sorted, and shipped to a trash dump. These keychains will market our company in a different way—to blue-collar workers. The keychains that make it will get packed into luggage, flown thousands of miles away, and then removed. Thinking about the reach of Bio Algorithms is mind boggling, but it all starts with the 100 keychains I hold in my hand, the 100 seeds that will never live together in this bag again.

Suddenly, my phone vibrates.

"Shit, I wanted to call my wife," I mumble.

I set the bag down and look at the screen. She just read my mind.

"Hello?" I say.

"Just *hello*? Where've you been all day?" Melissa says.

I can sense her offensive side. "Sorry, honey. It's just been a hectic day."

"Well, you usually call in the morning. Were you out late last night?" she asks.

Her voice causes me to stir. I have this secret in my mind, this shard of memories stored by my neurons. I wish I could find a way to purge these memories, to kill the neurons that hold the weight that weighs me down. If I were able to do this, I'd be a rich man. Perhaps, I can talk to our R&D department, or better yet, Venus. As I dither, I realize that I must respond.

"Uh, yeah. I mean no. I just stayed up looking over some charts. What have you been up to?"

I am technically not lying. I guess it's called not being straightforward. Can she tell? I need to stop thinking, stop over-analyzing.

"Just finished dinner. Joyce is over with Jimmy," she says.

I listen intently to my phone conversation through the convention chatter. The sound of my kids playing and laughing makes me smile. I miss their innocence. "Oh, that's great. They're probably all playing video games."

"Of course. Joyce is even playing."

"Hi, Michael," I can faintly hear.

"Things are productive here. It's a great networking opportunity. I've met some interesting characters so far."

"Like who?"

"I'll tell you all about this convention when I get back, honey."

"Hey, what would you say if I fly out? We can extend the trip. Maybe go see Hoover Dam or take a gondola ride at The Venetian."

Melissa paints a pretty picture in my mind. This might be the thing I need to remove myself from my transgressions. We could stay at a new hotel on the Strip and take a different path. I could start over. But just as my mind melts, there's something in the chaos in front of me. It's a snake in my pit. The creature slithers between business suits. My heart races. My breathing escalates. It's Rachel, wearing a feminine suit. Bringing my wife out here would be a bad idea. I need to forget Vegas after this trip and vow never to return.

"Uh, well, I have to get back to the office when this is over. I have to prepare follow-ups for some potential investors and—"

Rachel looks my way. I turn to avoid eye contact, but I think she saw me.

"And what?" Melissa asks.

Jackie smile at her. No, Jackie. Don't offer that woman your hand! But it's too late. Jackie shakes hands with her and begins talking. Rachel smiles as she eagerly listens to my subordinate's pitch about her CEO, about me—Michael Harris.

The phone still rests against my ear. "I have to run. Sorry. I'll call you later." I close the phone.

I freeze as both women interact. Rachel looks stunning. Her hair is up with those pencil things holding it in place. Her skin glows under the lights. While she talks, her breasts bounce at the top of her business suit. As I stare, Jackie turns and points my way. There's nowhere to hide, nowhere to change my appearance. I'm stuck.

Rachel follows Jackie's gesture, and then sees me. Her eyes go wide, and then she smirks. Jackie walks my way, leading the snake into my sanctuary.

"This is Mister Michael Harris, Bio Algorithms' Chief Executive Officer," Jackie says.

Rachel extends her hand. I roll with it, resting my hand inside her constriction.

"So nice to meet you, *Mister Harris*."

"She is interested in possibly investing in the company," Jackie continues.

"Thank you, Jackie. I'll take it from here."

With that, Jackie leaves me alone with the serpent.

"What are you doing here?" I whisper.

"Nice booth, Mister Harris. Or is it Jack?"

"Hey, this is Vegas. We're all someone different, right?"

She paints my suit with her fingertip, toying with me. "You're telling me?" She looks around my safe zone, and then glances over my shoulder. "What's back there?"

Before I can respond, my hand vibrates. At first, I think it's my muscles reacting to her venom, but then I realize it's my cell phone. The screen reads, "Home."

"I have to take this," I say.

"You have to take care of business in front of you first," she says.

I silence the device, placing it in my pocket.

"You're such the popular man. So, did you enjoy yourself last night?" she asks.

My mind opens in front of her. I think back to her breasts bouncing, her supple skin against my groin, her lips surrounding my cock. Blood rushes to my dick.

"It was unbelievable. I thought it was a dream. What time did you leave?" I ask.

"Early. You were sleeping like a baby. You up for an encore?"

An encore? I thought she would call me out for the liar that I am. I have to stop thinking!

"Uh, I don't think so," I exhale.

"Come on. This is Vegas. When you go home, this all never happened."

Rachel does have a point. I should just roll with the Vegas fantasy. It's okay to have a little fun when you're in Sin City; in fact, you must. Right?

"Okay, how about dinner?"

She smiles. "Are you going as Jack or Mister Harris?"

"Which do you prefer?"

"Whoever that man was in bed last night," she laughs.

"Where's your convention badge?" I ask.

"Right here," she replies, pointing at her cleavage.

"Excuse me, Mister Harris," Jackie says, offering me two stout businessmen.

I hope they're not more creatures ready to attack. They look like two lawyers from one of the billboards littering this town.

"I'll be right there, Jackie," I say.

I return my focus to the slippery snake in front of me.

"Do you have a rental?" Rachel asks.

"A *rental* what?"

"A rental cock... Silly, a rental *car*," she chuckles.

"No? Why?"

"Well, get one with a navigation system. I'll give you a tour. Pick me up in the same spot as last night. Eight o'clock."

"Okay, but you have to get the hell outta here now. You're going to get me busted," I say with wide eyes.

"See you tonight."

Rachel slinks away from my booth. While I watch her hips sway, it feels as if she wasn't even here, but then I feel a knot tighten in my gut and realize that she has left me with her bite."

"Sir?" Jackie asks.

I step toward her, regaining my composure.

"Any luck with her?" she asks.

The knot in my gut tightens further. "*What*?"

"With investing. Any luck?"

"No, she's in the wrong business."

I focus on the two businessmen.

"Gentlemen, this is Mister Harris," Jackie says.

As the men introduce themselves and give me their resume, I overhear a college-aged kid ask Tony, "Do you have any more keychains?"

18

I need to get out of this chaos. How does anybody breathe in this convention hall? My work is done for now. Michael was so surprised to see me. I love catching men with their pants down.

I near the door, a chubby man in a suit holds it for me.

"Nice suit," he says as I pass.

I smirk.

"What company are you with?" he continues.

I just keep going. Not a bad pick-up line, but I already have my date for the evening. I have a few hours to kill. What's a girl to do in Vegas for a few hours?

I hail a cab. Good, it's a female driver. I'm tired of all these dumb dudes trying to jump my bones.

"Where to?" the female driver asks as I enter.

I get a good look at her baggy clothes. She wears no makeup, even her short hair is flat, but I can't blame her; she's a cab driver.

"Uh… Where's a good place to go shopping?" I ask.

She glances in her rear-view. I catch her eyes for a moment.

"What ya inta?"

"Underwear. I could use a new bra and panties."

"Hot date tonight, huh?"

I grin.

"Fashion Show Mall's gud. Lots of prissy stuff there."

We pull out and leave the convention behind. A monorail speeds by above my head. Las Vegas has changed so much since I last visited. I remember coming out here with *him*. It was our first trip together. I'll never forget that trip. He drove me around in a convertible, showed me the desert, showed me love. I remember driving to some lakebed. We were only a few miles from Interstate 15, but we seemed to be on another planet. I remember us making love out there in the desert, alone, isolated, together.

The cab turns onto the Strip. Traffic slows us to a stop. Cars consume Las Vegas Boulevard. There is nowhere to go, nowhere to turn legally, but the cab flies around the mess by using the turning lane. I jostle around. We make a sharp turn into Circus Circus, and then spin onto Industrial Road. My whole body slides around. I knock over a pile of coupon books in the backseat.

"Sorry, dear," the cabby says.

"A little slower, please."

We pass Sapphire. The place looks different during the day. A Hispanic man is sweeping the parking lot. A train zips by on the side of the building. The place looks abandoned. Then, we pass a massage parlor that says, "Open 24 Hours" at the end of a strip mall. An exotic dancewear store is next to it. A billboard with a 20-foot stripper solicits us in front of the Can Can Room.

This is the seedy side of Sin City, the place breeding in the Strip's shadows.

I notice the cab driver studying me in the rear-view. She has this look about her in her comatose eyes, the kind of look that could get her stabbed in the county jail on a summer night.

"There's the Love Boutique," she says.

"That's nice," I reply.

"I bet a girl like yaself shops in there gud."

"There's a time and place for everything."

"Ya wanna do a little shoppin'? On me."

"What do you mean?" I furrow my brow.

"Let's have some fun. I'll lick ya pretty and use this." The cabby opens the glove box. A 10-inch mold of a fat cock glares at me.

"Just stop here, please," I say.

"Nevada law. We can't stop in the street."

I grab my cell phone.

"Listen, bitch. I don't fuck women. I have someone on the other end of this phone who will make you suffer. Should I call him?"

"No. Sorry, ma'am. The mall's right there."

We sit in silence as the entrance to the mall greets us.

"Saks Fifth Avenue is fine," I say.

She pulls into the taxi drop off. The meter reads "$12.25." I give her ten bucks.

"You lost the rest back there."

I jump out and don't look back. The Fashion Show Mall surrounds me with class. Any mall with Saks and Neiman Marcus is worth my walk. As I enter the guts of the mall, models stomp down a runway, bathed by spotlights and the eyes of a thousand shoppers. This is all Vegas.

I anticipate my night with Michael. I like this guy, not because I have to, but because I want to. He is corny. On paper, he comes off as some uptight CEO, but he's nothing more than a kid in a suit. He reminds me of…*him.*

I pass two girls selling T-shirts at a kiosk. The one wearing black looks like she is training the other girl.

"T-shirts…Hoover Dam…Las Vegas…Three for ten," she announces.

I keep walking. Another kiosk catches my eye. Purses made from candy wrappers are on display. It's a clever product, but too tacky for me. I need a store with some seductive class. In the distance is Victoria's Secret. While I wouldn't buy their cheap perfume, I'd buy their underwear.

What color does Michael like? I wore black last night, but black lingerie is best for the first encounter. It's a color that contains all colors, a favorite of any guy. As I walk into the store, I see a girl barely out of high school wearing a sweat suit.

"That's a nice purse," she says.

I glance at my little black handbag.

"It's a handbag, dear."

"We have a sale on perfume, seven for thirty-five."

"Not for me. I just want some lingerie."

"Sure," she says.

As I remove my eyes from her, I feel her hands on my chest.

"What are you doing?" I say.

"Just getting your measurements," she says, groping me with a tape measure.

"I know my measurements. Please, keep your hands to yourself."

"Sorry. I just want to make sure your girls are supported."

"Did you just call my breasts *girls*? This is why I don't come into this place."

I storm out of the store. I decide to get a yogurt smoothie and shop at Saks. I check out the lingerie and find something that should work—a matching set of red bra and panties. As I decide, an older saleswoman wearing a business suit approaches.

"That bra will give your breasts great support," she says.

I smile. "Thank you. I'd like to try it on."

"Right this way."

The 34-C bra fits snuggly and provides the proper lift. The small thong panties do their trick. I buy the items with a credit card. That's all that I've been using the past three months. As I walk outside the mall, I look at my watch. It's 5:00. I only have three hours left. I dread finding a suitable taxi. As I stand in the line, my cell phone rings. The Caller ID displays, "ka." My heart races as I pick up the phone.

19

The kids grab their overflowing yogurt cups and run toward the treat cart. I just want a taste of vanilla. I pull the handle, but my taste turns into a dessert.

"Mom, Ben put chocolate sprinkles on my yogurt," Sophia says, holding her cup, a few chocolate sprinkles covering the top.

"Ben, why did you put those in your sister's yogurt? You know she doesn't like the chocolate ones."

I scoop out the sprinkles with a spoon. "There. All better now."

"Aunt Melissa. Can I get chocolate syrup?" Jimmy asks.

"Just a little. You don't want to have bad dreams," I say.

"What?"

"Chocolate makes you have bad dreams. You never heard that?"

"Does vanilla give you good dreams?" he asks.

"Ha, that's a good question. I don't know. But you can have some chocolate. Go ahead."

I reach the cashier. Joyce joins us after having used the restroom.

"Are you sure you don't want any?" I ask Joyce.

"You know me," she says.

"Are these all together?" the teenage cashier asks.

"Yes. Put it all together," I say.

"I got it, sis. My treat," Joyce goes.

"No. Your money's no good when you're with me."

I pay with American Express.

"What do you say?" Joyce says to Jimmy.

"Thank you, Aunt Melissa," he responds.

"You're welcome."

We all sit down at a small table. The kids dive into their cups as if it were the last time they would ever have yogurt. For me, it is, at least that's what I keep saying.

"Slow down," I say to Ben and Sophia.

I taste the rich, creamy vanilla. It's smooth, silky. My taste buds sing. This is why the kids are shoveling it in.

"Are you sure you don't want a taste," I offer Joyce.

"I'm good."

A man in a suit walks in. He is tall, about 40-years-old, a briefcase in his hand. I signal with my eyes. Joyce shifts her focus. We talk in code like two Army snipers eyeing up a kill. She shakes her head. I squint my eyes.

"What are you doing, Mom?" Ben asks.

Joyce and I laugh.

"Me and your aunt are just playing a game."

"Can I play?"

"You eat your yogurt, kiddo, or a bird will come down and eat it all."

The kids laugh, and then focus on their taste buds.

"Why not?" I whisper to Joyce.

"Not my type."

"What is your type?"

"I haven't found it yet," my 40-year-old sister responds.

We laugh.

"You found Michael so fast after Doug," she says.

"Michael found me."

The guy in the suit grabs a cup and studies the yogurts. He's wearing a Calvin Klein suit. I can tell by the stitching around the collar. Michael has the same suit. The man glances our way. Joyce and I look at our kids.

"He just checked you out," Joyce mutters.

"No. He just checked *you* out," I clarify.

"Have you ever thought about it?" she asks.

"Thought about *what*?"

"You know. Behind Michael. If the chance presented itself," Joyce says.

"No. Never."

"Not even in the tens years? What if you knew he'd never find out?"

I think about her question. Sure, I look at men who I find attractive, but I am in love with my family, Michael being the central part.

"I guess that's the difference between you and me, sis. Stability is something that I would never trade for lust. When I was single and went to the mall alone, I would get lost. Now, when I'm alone in the mall, I look for my husband."

"I wish I had that. It sounds nice," she says.

"You will. Just give it time."

"I'm running out of time."

The door to the yogurt store opens. A striking woman enters wearing a business suit and a scarf. She is an island woman, classy and cool. She glides to the handsome man and embraces him with a kiss.

"That right there is the real question," Joyce says.

"What do you mean?"

"If given the opportunity, would Michael cheat?"

I know Michael. He is a good father and a good husband. I wish he were here, with me, with us.

20

This Mustang GT is fast. I told the kid that I wanted something with flash, but he gave me a rocket. It's "7:59" on the dash clock. The Hilton is towering up ahead. I punch the gas; the V8 under the hood sucks in air. The force pushes my body against the seat as the open air flows through my hair.

I arrive at the meeting point at exactly 8:00. I put the car into park and leave the engine humming. All I see are the two palm trees guarding the side entrance. I flip down the mirrors, check my clean-shaven face, and then put my hand through my slicked hair. It glides through without restriction because my ring is in my pocket.

"Are you picking up?"

I look around for the slippery voice. She's behind me. How did she sneak up on me? I jump out of the car and behold the electrifying woman in front of me. Her skin is radiating. Tonight she's wearing black. Her cocktail dress hugs her frame. It starts low and ends high, a red bra peeking out. Why would she wear a red bra under a black dress? But the look in her eyes answers my question. I am nervous even though I've been inside her. I lean in as she presses her lips against mine, her aroma arresting me.

"You look stunning," I say.

"You the same, Mister Harris."

"Where to?" I ask.

"Let's see where the road takes us."

We launch from our spot, the tires chirping. We speed down the Strip. It's a wonderful night in the desert. Rachel and I take it all in. Everything is energized, so full of life. We speed past the Riviera. That's the hotel from the movie *Casino*. We see the Fashion Show Mall and Caesars Palace. People march on the streets. A group of women pierces the pavement with their heels; a young black guy hands out CDs; a woman with a shaved head dances on the sidewalk. I think I see that black woman again walking in the crowd. She's wearing a red mini-dress, which complements her African black skin. I take my foot off the throttle to get a better look, but it's too late. We pass her.

We sit at the traffic light at Flamingo Road. We have a perfect view of the Bellagio Fountains. They dance and spin to Sinatra's "Fly Me to the Moon." Rachel and I stare, bonded by the beautiful sight. The water reaches for the desert sky. I look over and see a tear in her eye. Why does she cry?

"What's the matter?" I ask.

"Nothing. It's just dust."

She grabs a napkin and hides her face. The light turns green. I accelerate past the water.

"Are you hungry?" she asks.

"Famished."

"Well, I have a place for you. Make a right on Tropicana."

I follow her directions. We pass The Orleans, turn some more, and then pass the Rio.

"Where are we going?" I ask.

"We're almost there."

Finally, we turn onto Spring Mountain Road. The Strip is in the distance. As we drive, the English signs turn Oriental; the Spanish roofs add Asian accents; the attorneys on the billboards look like cast members from a Kung Fu film.

"Make a right here?" she says.

"Where are we?"

"Welcome to Chinatown."

I park the car and open the passenger side door for her. As she steps out with black daggers on her feet, the lights make love to her legs. I feel so young again.

We walk toward a strip mall. Symbols from Asian languages are everywhere. I see a hairdresser, a tea bar, a coffee shop, and a place called "Happy Massage" with a bright sign reading "Open." We walk by a restaurant; several Asian men are smoking and laughing outside. We pass a locker filled with cooked ducks.

"Which place are you taking me?"

"We're here."

I look at the blacked-out windows. Symbols I can't read are scribbled on the front. "Japanese Fusion" is scripted in fancy font on the door. I can't tell whether the place is some front for an es-cort service or a place to eat, or perhaps it's a fusion of both.

I open the door; the smell of mothballs hits me. Dim lights cast the restaurant in tranquility. Several couples dine at tables. Asian servers scamper. A bar sits on the side with exotic dishes moving on a conveyor belt. As we approach the check-in podium, it looks as if we are the only two patrons born in North America, but then again, my date is full of surprises.

"We're not in Kansas anymore, Toto," I whisper.

"Best Japanese food in Vegas."

"Isn't this *China*-town?"

"Hello. Dinner for two?" a frail Asian man asks.

"Yeah," I respond. I look at Rachel. "If this is dinner?"

"Table. This way," he says, leading us into the maze.

We each take a seat at a table. Another Asian server, one who is even frailer, hands us two menus. The nail on his pinky finger is an inch long. Inside the menu, there are symbols everywhere, a treasure map in a foreign language.

"What? No English?"

"No, no English. Japanese," he says.

I glance at Rachel; a coy smile covers her face.

I point to a symbol that looks like a radio antenna.

"What is this?"

The server smiles.

"Mmm... That...*ooottooo...ooottooo.*"

"What are you saying?" I ask.

"I draw."

He pinches his finger and thumb while moving his hand. This I understand as the international sign of drawing. I reach into my suit and grab a Bio Algorithms pen and a business card— Jack's business card. The Asian server takes the tools and sketches something on the back of the card. I humor him. He draws five tentacles and a circle connecting them.

"Octopus?" I say.

"Yes. Yes. Two dishes?" he asks, smiling.

I look at Rachel. Octopus is not a regular meal I eat at home, but I'm far, far away from home. Rachel smiles, nods at the server, and hands him her menu. He grabs mine, and then takes off as if an immigration agent has walked through the door.

"And sake," she says as he trails away.

"What have you got me into?" I say to Rachel.

All she does is smile. I look around the table.

"Shit, he took that business card and my pen."

"We'll take it out of his tip," she replies.

I shrug. It's nice to rid that middleman named Jack from my trip; he was weighing me down. All I care about now is to enjoy myself, to give my time and my attention to individuals I choose. The woman in front of me is one of those individuals. She has made this trip both terrifying and exciting. She has made me a better man. At least that is what I'm trying to convince myself.

"So, the secret's out of the bag. What do you do?" she says.

"I work on the East Coast."

"Ohio, right?"

"No, Philadelphia."

"You're running out of strikes, mister," she replies.

I'm tired of lying, but at the same time, tired of the serious questions. "I'll let you take it out of my tip."

"Oh, look who's coming around."

"This is totally not me," I say.

"Well in Vegas, you can be anybody you want. This town is a living, breathing character. The moment you step off the plane you feel the energy, the heartbeat that keeps this place alive."

"It's amazing to fly in, seeing the barren desert for miles and miles. Then Vegas just sneaks up on you," I say.

"Well, the desert will bite you in the back if you're not careful. Don't forget that."

Her words cause me to hold my breath. Rachel has many thoughts, many emotions, that grab me when I least expect. While

I have only known her for 24 hours, she has given me things to ponder for years to come.

"So, what exactly is your company?" she asks.

"We research and develop computer algorithms."

"Right over my head," she replies, acting out the motion.

"You've played video games, right?"

"Hell yeah, I love that sports game with the little characters. Especially the tennis."

"Well, how do you think the computer knows how to play against you?"

"I don't know, but Mario usually beats me."

"Mario is a computer algorithm designed by computer scientists."

"Games? Is that what you do?"

"Yes, but on a much higher scale. I'm talking robotics, artificial intelligence, self-learning."

"Again with the geek speak."

"I know. It's in my blood."

As Venus fills my mind, my blood, I feel something tickling my pants. At first, I account it to my tie, but then the tickle turns into a massage. I glance down; there are five toes, nails painted with black nail polish, rolling and rubbing my groin. I bite my lip.

"Well, I think it's sexy," she exhales.

A shadow enters the corner of my eye. I clear my throat. She recoils. Yet another Asian server arrives. He has a prominent tattoo of a yin-yang on his forearm that his white chef shirt fails to cover. He sets down two cups and a white bottle with a spout. I assume it's sake. Just as fast, the server puts two dishes in front of us. Back home, I'd have a plate of pasta drenched in Marinara sauce with a piece of sourdough bread. But in front of me, I see a plate of ooey gooey tentacles covered in suction cups. How am I going to eat this?

Everything happens in slow motion. The Asian server drops us some chopsticks. Rachel pours us two cups of sake. She pushes one in front of me.

"Eat up. You'll need all the energy tonight," she says.

Rachel raises her cup. I break my trance and raise mine. This trip has been full of new experiences. We clank cups.

"Cheers," Rachel says.

As we drink up the sake, my fears subside. Alcohol is a wonder drug. I take down three shots before I muster the courage to taste the creature of the sea. It's slimy, rubbery, and does *not* taste like chicken. As we joke and we laugh, I feel a sensation in my pants. This time it's in my pocket. As Rachel pours us another round, I reach in and silence my cell phone.

"Tell me something interesting," Rachel asks.

"Something interesting… Let's see. Well, I have a pet peeve. I hate long voicemail greetings."

"What do you mean?"

"You know. People who record their own messages. Like…'Hi. You've reached Michael Harris, Chief Executive Officer of Bio Algorithms. I'm so terribly sorry that I've missed your call. I am either out of the office, away from my desk, or simply don't want to talk. But if you please leave your name, number, brief message, or long, I will return your call. Or maybe I won't. Thank you. Good bye and good luck.'"

"Ha! That is longwinded."

"Tell me about it. But I've heard so many people with variations of that. But all the people who get that message have to wait twenty seconds each time to get to the beep."

"Twenty seconds, oh no!" she replies, sarcastically.

"Just do the math."

"I'll let *you* do the math."

"If I call this person every day and have to leave five voicemails a week. That's one hundred seconds a week. Times this by fifty-two weeks in a year, that's fifty two hundred seconds. That is roughly…what…ninety minutes a year or an hour and a half of just wasting time."

"But what if you take a week vacation?" she says.

I grin. "No. Just hear me out."

She smirks, shaking her head. "Okay. Well you're right. That's a lot of time, Mister Harris. What do you suggest?"

"Just give something short and sweet. Like 'You've reached the voicemail of Michael Harris. Please leave a message.'"

"I like that better."

"That takes five seconds to hear, which divides our long message by four. So, instead of wasting an hour and a half a year, we only wait a little over twenty minutes."

"You should write a paper on this."

"No. I'm just saying."

"You okay here?" the tattooed Asian server asks.

"Another sake," Rachel says, sending the man scurrying.

"So you tell me something interesting," I say.

"Hmm, I'm not that interesting," Rachel says.

She blushes and removes her eyes from me for a moment, just long enough to know that I'm breaking through her shield. Either that or it's the sake.

"Tell me about your family heritage. Where are you from?" I ask.

"I don't know. Where are you from?"

"Well, my dad's side of the family is Irish and my mom's is from Poland."

"Interesting mix."

The Asian server arrives with another bottle.

"You like?" he says, pointing to my half-eaten plate.

"It's different. I'll give you that."

He chuckles, and then rushes away.

"So, you're good at turning the conversation around," I say, smiling.

"That's my specialty." She presses her red lips together.

I pour another sake. I watch her grip the little cup with her fingers, nails painted in red. She accepts my pour, brings the cup to her lips, and then lets the liquid enter her mouth. Her throat muscles clench, and then the liquid enters her belly. As she removes the cup, I catch her eyes. They are moist as the soft lighting bounces off them. A single tear teeters on her eyelid, and then falls like a petal from a red rose. It glides down her cheek chaotically across the pores of her face, until she stops it with her finger.

"What's wrong?" I ask.

She looks at me as a different person, one who breathes more life than lust.

"I have a secret to tell you," she says.

A knot twists in my gut. Does she know about my family, my wife? Does she know something about me that I don't?

"I've been to Vegas before. About five years ago."

"Well, that's nothing to hide."

"Wait. Just let me finish," she interjects. "You remind me a lot of my...*husband*. He took me to Vegas five years ago. We had the time of our lives. He showed me the desert, the lights, the entertainment. He showed me love, as we got married at a chapel near the Stratosphere. We were planning to start a family, a life together, but then shortly after we got back home to New York, something happened... It was a dark night. We were driving. I keep replaying it in my mind. I saw the lights first. I tried to warn him, but it happened so fast. We both weren't wearing our seatbelts, and he jumped on me to save me in the car. He was killed instantly…right in front of me."

Rachel breaks down. I give her an extra napkin. What should I do? Should I stand? Should I scoot my chair closer to her? Her story makes me think about Melissa and our trip together to Vegas. It also makes me think about that time 5 years ago, that time she passed out from dehydration when hiking. I had held her comatose body in my arms, without water, without a phone, without a way to save my wife. We were all alone out there. If it hadn't been for that other hiker, I may be telling the same story to Rachel.

"I'm sorry. I don't know why I told you that. I barely know you," Rachel says.

"It's okay. Do you want to go?" I ask.

"No. It's fine. Just forget it. Let's have a good time. We're only here for a few days."

"When do you go back?"

"Soon," she says.

Suddenly, my stomach turns sour. It gurgles, yelling at me, scolding me for filling it with a foreign substance.

"What's wrong?" Rachel asks.

"I don't feel so hot."

I sense my stomach muscles working backwards. I bolt toward the restroom. Both Asian servers are looking at me. The one with the tattoo points me toward the right door. I punch open the men's room and reach a stall. And then like that, the octopus expels into the toilet.

After vomiting the last half hour's worth of food, I clean up, and then rejoin Rachel.

"Are you okay?" she asks.

"Yeah. I'm better now."

"I'm sorry for bringing you here."

"No, don't be sorry. I had the choice to come."

I pay the bill and grab a business card from the restaurant. Just in case I get food poisoning, I need to know where I got it. We head back to the Hilton. She caresses my leg in the car as we drive, taking in the lights. I feel better. I crave the rest of the night; I crave this woman. As we wait for the elevator in the hotel, she rubs my back and fixes my tie.

"Feeling better?" she asks.

"Still not a hundred percent."

"Don't worry. I'll make you a new man."

I bump against the "down" arrow, lighting it.

"Are you taking us to the basement to strangle me?" Rachel jokes.

I laugh. We enter the elevator that is going up.

"Nineteen, right?" Rachel asks.

"Uh, no, it's twenty nine now." I press the number on the grid.

"What? You have *two* rooms?"

"No, I switched to another one."

"You scared I might come back?"

I blush.

"Sweetie, you're in too deep with me," she says.

I lead Rachel to my new room. We enter and undress each other. This time it's slower, more intense. We indulge in foreplay longer this time, and then fuck like old lovers.

21

I'm sitting here listening to Michael tell me his theory on voicemail. He is so geeky, but geeky in an interesting way. He's several men rolled up in one—a confident executive, a voracious love maker, and a computer geek. He has the look of Gordon Gekko at one angle, but then in another, I can see Bud Fox. It seems that the alcohol is awakening his playful side. I like the way he talks, the way he moves his mouth when he speaks fast, and the dimple that forms when he grins. He reminds me so much of the man in my dreams.

"You okay here?" the tattooed Asian server asks.

"Another sake," I say, sending him scurrying.

"So you tell me something interesting," he says.

"Hmm, I'm not that interesting," I say.

Michael asks me about my family heritage, but I divert the question. While he seems to be opening up to me, I can't. I hold a deep dark secret that only one other individual knows. But the more I talk to Michael, and the more images he paints in my mind, a knot tightens in my belly. Can I go through with this? I've done bad things with my life since *he* has passed, things that I can never admit, unless forced to do so.

More sake arrives at the table. Michael interacts with the server. I watch the way Michael's eyes go wide at his plate, the comical language barrier between him and the server. I study Michael's hair, his green eyes, his defined face. Michael looks just like my love the first time I came here five years ago. I even think we sat at this same table. I must say something or this will eat me from the inside.

Michael pours me another cup of sake. The heat from the alcohol warms my fingers. I move the cup toward my mouth and take a sip. It tickles my taste buds, and then I clench my throat and swallow the mixture. As the liquid enters my belly, my mind overwhelms with guilt. I feel a tear form on my eye. It's too late to hide. I look at Michael as the tear falls down my face.

"What's wrong?" he asks.

I look at Michael as I had looked at my love.

"I have a secret to tell you," I say.

I tell Michael about the incident that keeps me awake at night, that hurts my head like a dull headache, that has made me give up on my life. I tell him because I want to tell him, not because it's some made up story or part of my job. There was something about Michael that drew me to him after seeing him on the cover of that magazine, something that I knew would test me. Opening up to him makes me feel better. I haven't told anyone this story since escaping New York after that tragedy.

It feels good to cry. Michael tries to offer his hand, but it's okay. I don't want him to do anything other than listen.

Michael suddenly gets sick. He takes off to the restroom. I feel awful for bringing him here, awful because it was only for me. As Michael takes his time, I think about him. Can I really go through with what's about to happen? I feel bad for him not because I told him a secret, but because I only told him one.

We go back to the hotel. I let myself return to the flirtatious girl who always has fun, always knows what to say and how to say it. As we wait in line for the elevator, I see a short woman with almond eyes. She looks at me as if she knows me, or maybe it's Michael. Even though his head is down, he seems to be feeling better. We enter the elevator and go up to his new room. I feel closer to him now and want nothing more than to make love to him. I work on him slowly, intently. I suck his cock not because it makes him feel good, but because it makes me feel good.

Michael takes his time with me. He is full of passion. He runs his fingers across my skin as if I'm a piece of art that he is painting. I ride Michael slowly, feeling his cock rub me deep inside. I orgasm twice tonight.

Afterwards, I lie on his chest and listen to his heart beating. It sounds slower than last night, more relaxed. I fall asleep quickly and dream of my father taking me, his seven-year-old daughter, to the Philadelphia Zoo.

22

The water is cold. I turn the dial even farther to the left, but the water isn't hot enough. Should I wash my hair? I washed it yesterday. The whole process is just so much work. Michael is still away. I don't have anything planned tomorrow except to take the kids shopping for new shoes. I grab the Pantene bottle.

"For normal to oily hair," I read aloud.

It's almost out. I should buy more of this tomorrow at the store, but I always forget. By the time I get out of the shower, the thought of more shampoo will be out of my mind. I wish I could make a list in here. Do they sell a waterproof notepad, or even a whiteboard? If they don't, I should invent one. I know it would be a great seller. Maybe Michael could design it. I should tell him about it.

As I dawdle, I squeeze the bottle, sending a glob of shampoo into my palm. Why did I just do that? I said that I didn't want to wash my hair tonight, but as I thought about buying more shampoo, instinct kicked in. What should I do with this? If I put it back into the bottle, then water will get inside. I don't think that's good. It might dilute the shampoo. But I suppose it will dilute anyway when I put it in my hair. I don't really want to wash my hair. I just want to end this shower. I let the shampoo wash down the drain. Now I really have to buy more shampoo.

My mind hurts. I wish Michael were here. I miss him. I wish he would call me. He was rude before. But, I know he's busy. I can't wait to hear about his trip when he returns.

I step out of the shower, dry myself, and get ready for bed. The house is quiet and chilly. I tiptoe to Ben's room and peek inside. He is sleeping with his basketball sheets on his twin bed. I watch his chest rise, rhythmically. I hope he is off in a happy dream. I leave his door open a crack, and then creep to Sophia's room. As my eyes adjust to the darkness, I see my daughter tucked under her colorful flower covers.

She moves. "Dad?" she asks.

"No. It's only me, sweetie," I say.

She sits up. I gravitate toward her and sit down. She is sweating.

"What's wrong?" I ask.

"I had a bad dream."

"Aww, I'm sorry, sweetie. It's okay now. Mom's here."

I wipe her brow and comb her hair with my fingers.

"When is Dad coming back?"

"The day after tomorrow. Go back to sleep now, sweetie."

"Can you lay with me?"

"Of course."

It's "10:38" on her clock. I position her in the twin bed as I lie beside her. She is warm inside my arms. I feel her heart beating against my body. Her warm breath tickles the little hairs on my arm. My chill has subsided. I feel warm, contented. As I listen to the sound of silence, I drift away into a dream.

I am back at the yogurt store earlier this evening. Everyone is eating yogurt except for me. Ben, Sophia, and Jimmy indulge in their cups. Joyce is even eating yogurt. I am craving a taste.

"Can I have some?" I ask my family.

They ignore me.

"Hello?" I say.

Am I even here? I touch Ben's face, but my hand whips back on instinct. He's freezing! "Ben, you're so cold."

He ignores me. I reach for Sophia, but my hand freezes as soon as it touches her. "Sophia, it's Mom!"

I extend my hand to Jimmy and Joyce, but they feel like ice from the darkest part of the South Pole.

"What's happening?"

The crowd keeps eating their yogurts. Suddenly, the door opens. A man with a trench coat enters. I remember him. He has a shaved head and pale, lifeless skin. His face is visible, a face with arched eyebrows and eyes burning red. I try to get up, but I can't.

"Kids. Come on. Let's go," I say, but they ignore me. "Joyce!"

The man walks over and grabs a yogurt cup. He pulls a lever. Blood pours out and fills the cup. The door opens again. It's a woman in a red mini-dress. As she scans the room, I notice blood covering her hands. I try to scream, but I can't. I try to move, but I'm frozen. The woman and the man meet in the middle of the store, and then kiss.

After they embrace, they look at me. They walk closer, the man holding the cup of blood. My heart yells; my mind pounds.

The man and the woman take a spoon and offer Ben and Sophia the blood. My kids look at it and open their mouths.

"No! No! Nooo!"

I jar awake. Sophia is sleeping placidly next to me. The clock reads, "11:53." It was all a dream. I tuck in Sophia. Then, I sneak to the door and watch my daughter sleep. I leave the door open a crack before heading to my room. My master bedroom greets me, but it's cold in here. I fill my lungs with isolation. I feel lonely. It's one thing to be single and alone, but it's another to be alone and married. I'm going to call Michael.

I speed dial him on my cell phone. I listen to the first ring, anticipating the signal beaming across the United States into the Mojave Desert. The phone rings again, and again. I wait for a click, a snippet of sound that signals someone picking up. But all I get is another ring.

I hear a noise. I raise my head an inch.

"Hello, this is Michael…"

At first, I prepare to talk to my other half, to hear him ask me how I am, but I am only fooling myself. This is the sound of his contrived voice.

"…sorry that I missed your call. I am either away from my phone or on another line. If you please leave a detailed message, I will be sure to return your call. Thanks."

His message is dreadfully long, too long. I hang up before the beep. I am sure Michael will see the missed call, or at least I hope he will.

I place the phone back on the nightstand, and then shut off the lights in my room. I lie here in the darkness, feeling cold and restless. I keep my eyes open, but I only see black. I fill the room with a whisper, "Michael, can you hear me?"

23

The sun warms my face. I open my eyes. I must have been asleep. I feel so refreshed. It feels late. Wow. I slept like a baby. What did I do last night? I'm naked. My balls ache. I have a moment of confusion, a moment right after you wake where the line between dream and reality blurs. Suddenly, images of Rachel flood my mind. I can feel her smooth skin, taste her sweetness, smell her aroma. But no one is next to me; there's just an imprint of where she had slept. I caress the white sheet. It's still warm. This is the second morning that she has abandoned me.

"I'm not letting you go that easy," she says from somewhere.

I look toward her voice. In the morning sunlight, I see Rachel's body covered by only a towel, which pushes up her breasts. The cotton rests just above her nipples. I smile. She saunters my way and kisses me. There's a red reflection in her eyes. Are they glowing red? Then I realize it's only the clock. It's "7:55."

"Oh, shit. It's late. I have to get downstairs," I say, springing up.

"Downstairs? You have your henchmen doing the legwork."

My underwear is on the desk in front of the mirror. "I know, but I should be down there," I say.

"Come on. Let's spend the day together. We can do the Strip."

"I don't know. Tomorrow's the last day. I need to glean some more investors."

"Let your bubbly booth girl do the gleaning, whatever that means."

"Jackie… She's such a hard worker."

"See, she'll cover you."

I glance at myself in the mirror. Stubble covers my face; my hair is a mess; the color red smudges my cheeks. My eyes focus on the creature in my room. Her freshness energizes me like morning coffee. Whom am I kidding? I am the Chief Executive Officer, the man at the top. I need to delegate tasks more, to have faith in my staff.

Rachel approaches me with her hypnotic sway. I freeze, as I can't look away. As she nears me, the towel falls. She has made up my mind for me. She pushes me on the bed. My penis fills with blood as she kisses her way down to it. The morning sun bathes her naked body. I anticipate her mouth. She kisses my dick, toying with me.

"Suck it. Come on. Put your lips around it," I whisper to myself.

I clench it, feeling my racing heartbeat. As her damp hair tickles my stomach, she takes my cock in her mouth. She sucks and squeezes with her lips. My mind melts as my title strips away. I'm nothing more than an animal, giving in to the most primitive instinct. Women have such power over men. We love them, loathe them, crave them, and hate them…sometimes all at the same time. I wonder whether she wants me to service her, but it seems that she only wants me to come. I listen to my libido, focus on her lips, her tongue, the warmth inside her mouth. I near my orgasm. My groin pulls my balls up. I take a deep breath and feel the pressure. My toes wiggle. Then, I explode in her mouth, spasm after spasm. She swallows it all. I just lie here like mush. She comes up and kisses my mouth. I can taste the remnants of my own cum.

"How was that, Mister Chief Executive?"

"You're going to be the end of me," I respond, grinning.

She laughs.

"Let me go down and tell my staff to cover," I say.

I spring from my spot and shower, shave, and don a white dress shirt, black & white tie, and a black suit. Rachel finishes her bathroom routine as I head to the convention to cook the books. As I take the elevator down, I have time to myself, have time to think, have time to reflect. Who is Rachel? How did I meet her? It seemed to have happened by chance, yet it didn't. She has opened my mind to a side that I never knew I had, a side that I plan to take back to PA to use to grow my relationship with Melissa. As I verbalize my wife's name in my mind, a knot constricts in my core. How did I cheat on her? *Why* did I cheat on her? I may never know the answers to these questions, but I realize that this city has a power unlike anything I have ever experienced. I realize that I haven't talked to Melissa since yesterday, and even then, we ended our conversation abruptly. As I walk through the casino at the Hilton, I reach for my phone. It's not there. I stop to check the pockets in my slacks and my jacket. An old woman nearly double my age at a blackjack table stares at me. My phone must be in my other pants. Will it be okay up there with her? I'm sure it will be. I shrug at the woman; she takes a puff from her cigarette.

I flash my badge to the guard and enter the convention. The place is less busy today. Perhaps the other businessmen have found their own Rachels.

A bubbly girl offers me a card.

"Have you donated blood yet? We still have our blood drive going on," she says.

"No, thanks," I say, respectfully refusing the card.

As I near my booth, Jackie and Tony are at the front. It feels good to have workers who step up and manage themselves. I notice them talking. I slow down before they see me in order to eavesdrop. Are they talking about their boss?

"Green Valley Ranch was great," Tony says.

"I told you, it reminds me of Florida," Jackie replies.

Tony leans in and steals a kiss from Jackie. "And you looked so sexy in that bikini," he says.

"I thought you liked me better with it off?"

So, this is how my employees act when I'm not around. I guess I can't blame them. I continue my stroll with a smile.

"Someone's happy this morning," Jackie says.

"I bet you just spoke with your wife," Tony says.

Don't remind me, Tony. "Uh, well, something has come up. Can you both cover the booth all day?" I say.

"Is anything wrong?" Jackie asks.

"No, actually, I've just been invited to play golf with some potential investors. You know how most business is done on the golf course," I lie.

"Okay, we can cover. No problem. We have our pitch down," Jackie says.

"And plenty of keychains," Tony adds.

"Good," I reply.

As my two brightest marketers man their posts, I glance around my booth. I see extra bags of keychains and trinkets. I look at the flyers attracting investors. I analyze the large lock on the door to the back room. This is my safe haven, my home away from home. This booth is something that this city did not create; I created it back in the mountainous Northeast. I think about my job, my degrees, my time at Penn State. My favorite professor during college taught my Algorithms & Data Structures class. He told me that while it is important to use logic to solve problems, it is even more important to use logic to prevent problems. I look at the computer monitor on display to my right and see a video of Venus performing open heart surgery.

24

I can still taste him in my mouth. He's saltier than the men I've had. Maybe it was the octopus from last night finding its way out through his semen. I look at myself in the mirror. This hair is not cooperating today. I just washed it, yet it's like I just got out of the pool. It must be the chlorine in the water at these hotels. Why do they have to put so much chlorine in? I could even taste it on Michael's dick when I was giving him a blowjob. I didn't tell him that. I didn't want him to lose his erection. I wonder how long Michael will be. I should just take another shower. This time I will use the whole bottle of conditioner.

I run the water again. It's still as warm as my shower 30 minutes ago. I remove my towel and step inside. The water feels refreshing as I let it flow over me. I check my legs, my underarms, my pussy. All feel smooth, just as they did 30 minutes ago. It's an action ingrained in me every time I step under water.

As I dump the small complimentary bottle of conditioner into my hand and massage it into my hair, I wait…and wait. I figure I will wait at least five minutes. I want to make sure it works this time. A busy day is in front of me. Where will Michael take me? I want to see the Strip and how much it has changed. I want to get lost with Michael, relive memories in my mind. I'm using him just as he's using me.

A ring sounds, stopping me like a cat hearing a truck pass. I listen through the sound of the water. It's my phone in my bag on the bathroom counter. I step out of the shower, the water dripping from my hairless skin. The ring sounds again. I know who it is, but why is he calling me now? What if I am with Michael? Suppose Michael picked up.

"Yeah," I say into the phone.

"We do this today," the male voice instructs.

"Are you sure?"

"It has to be done today."

I pause, speechless.

"Just as we planned," the voice says.

I stand mute, staring in the mirror at the water beading on my breasts.

"*Okaaaay*?" the voice says.

"Okay," I finally respond.

I close the phone. Water vapor clings to the mirror. I wipe it and stare at the woman in front of me. She is someone I don't know, someone who changes every time I look at her. I stare at her pointed nipples, the tiny scar above her lip, her drenched hair. The woman in front of me lacks eyeliner, lacks blush, lacks lipstick. She is who she is. The weight of the task in front of me hits me hard. But why am I fooling myself? I came here for a reason. I knew that going in. But Michael is different. A part of me can't hurt the man I crave. It's like I'm hurting my love. But I think of the other end of the equation and smile. It's strictly business.

25

I exit the back room holding a duffel bag. I feel like a criminal in my own booth. Why?

"Oh, I thought you left," Jackie says.

"I'm leaving now. I'll have my cell phone on if you need me," I offer. "See you, Tony."

Tony smiles.

As I walk onto the floor, I smell cookies. Yes, chocolate chip cookies. Who would be baking cookies? I look at the booth across from me and see a thousand computer cables on a table. The booth next to it has a display of network switches. Then there's the booth next to me showing the language filtering software. Which one is baking cookies?

Suddenly, my duffel bag bumps into someone. My eyes see the disheveled suit of a man. I stop and catch his face. It's someone I least expect—Jack.

"Whoa. Watch that thing," Jack says, checking his knee. "Hey, mate. Long time no see."

His head looks freshly shaven, reflecting the intense lights. He looks clean, but his suit is still ruffled.

"Jack, you're always right around the corner. How's your client list shaping up?" I ask.

"Great. I'm so close to snagging a huge deal."

"Do I know the company?"

"It's all hush-hush right now, you know how it is. But you'll soon find out."

I really don't care about this guy. He has the worst timing. Was he watching me? I always bump into him at my booth. I wish I could crack his skull and see what his problem is. But that would require touching him.

He looks down at my duffel bag. "You look like you're a man on a mission."

"Just business meetings."

"Business meetings my ass. You met someone, didn't you? You can trust me, mate."

I take a gulp. That winning personality surfaces again. "No, it's strictly business," I say.

"Well, whoever she is, good for you. Show her a good time."

"See ya, Jack."

I move past him, his aftershave hitting me.

"You have my card. It's our last night. Use it," he says, trailing away.

As I turn the corner down another aisle, I think of nothing more than the woman waiting for me. I take the elevator up and move to my room. I insert my key slowly, grip the handle, and then turn it little by little to minimize the click. I want to see what she's doing, to catch her in a moment where she still thinks she is alone. I smell water vapor. Is that the shower? I thought she already took a shower. Perhaps she didn't like the taste of my cum. Wait… The sound is from the sink running.

I tiptoe inside the room and head to the hotel safe. I read the instructions and set the code to "2394." As I fumble with it, the sink turns off. Quickly, I jam the duffel bag inside.

"Is that you?" Rachel says from inside the bathroom.

"Yeah, you almost ready?"

I lock the safe, and then stand up.

"The question is *are you ready*?" I hear from behind me.

As I turn, my eyes fill with the five-foot-six-inch creature. Her feet stand on smaller heels as black slacks start at the ankles. She wears a red blouse, my favorite color, which hides the parts that roll around in my mind. She looks hip, ready for a cruise down the Strip. She steps closer as the sun catches her hair showing its volume and texture.

"Wow," I exhale.

"You're going to keep the suit on? It's going to be a hundred degrees the next two days."

"A good businessman never leaves home without a suit."

She comes closer and pulls my tie. "It just means more clothes I have to take off you."

I grab her waist and thrust her close. Her scent invigorates me. I kiss her intensely in a way that I haven't kissed since that time in college. Part of me wants to stay inside the room all day and fuck like rabbits. But another part wants to see Las Vegas and how much it has changed.

"Let me touch this up," Rachel says, referring to her lipstick.

I grab my cell phone from my pants pocket. Should I call Melissa now? No, it's too close for comfort.

Rachel shows me her lovely lips.

"What is the name of that? I love that color," I ask.

"Forbidden Red."

We head downstairs. As we walk off the elevator, an elderly couple walks on. I need to take care of this. I stop.

"What's wrong?" Rachel asks.

"I need to make a phone call."

"Is it—"

"Give me a minute," I interject.

I turn on my phone and look at the bakery café across from us—the perfect spot. As I wait for the device to wake, it flashes the dreaded battery sign, and then dies. I exhale.

"Batteries?" Rachel asks.

"Must be. I left my charger in the room."

"Don't worry about it. The phone will just get in the way."

I hesitate. I should really head up to the room and call her. Only a five-minute detour, and then I can enjoy the day. As I eye the elevator, Rachel's claw caresses my back. I focus on the muscles around my spine, the way they melt in her hand.

"Let's see Vegas," she says.

And then like that, I give in to the temptation. I drive us to Treasure Island. This seems like a good spot to start the day. Rachel and I meander around the casino and find our way outside to watch the pirate show. Scantily clad sirens mixed in with a few pirates jump, swirl, tumble, and whirl to the flashes and lights. The show is great with an appeal to everyone from a kid in a stroller to a grandfather with a walker. The best part is that it's free.

We walk across the street to The Venetian. The place is fit for a king and queen on vacation. The sidewalk in front sprawls across the property with wrought-iron fences, fountains, and sculpted concrete. Signs for the Asian club Tao catch our attention. Why is there an Asian attraction at an Italian-themed property?

Rachel and I sit in front and watch the gondolas.

"You can tell this is private property," I say to her.

"How do you know?"

"The sidewalk is sculpted and there is no trash. The city would not keep it this clean."

"I think it's great. Why don't the other casinos do that?" she says.

"It costs money to own more property. Money makes the world go 'round."

"Let's take a gondola ride," Rachel says.

I smile and walk her to our awaiting ride. The gondolier is a burly man who looks as if he is going to tip over the boat. But he knows how to position himself to make our ride smooth and sensual. His voice is deep as he sings to us. I don't know why I didn't take a ride before, but I realize that this probably wasn't even here when I had last flown into town.

Afterwards, we find our way back to the car and grab a bite to eat in the Fashion Show Mall. The place is full of class, and I can tell Rachel fits right in. As we share a pizza at an Italian eatery, the waiter offers us the honeymoon special for dessert. We don't get it.

After our late lunch, we decide to visit the Bellagio. The resort oozes modern luxury even though it's over 10 years old. Rachel and I peruse the Conservatory before heading outside to the Fountains. As we wait for the next show, a retired postal worker from Phoenix explains that there are 1,200 nozzles that spurt water. He enlightens us with the fact that the water can shoot into the air over 400 feet. Once the first water sprays, a dancing water show to "Luck Be a Lady" captivates us. What a fitting song.

I hold Rachel and kiss her softly as the water sings and the music dances. I feel so alive, so energized. I hug Rachel tightly. I can feel her heart beating. It's different than I remember; it's beating faster and more forcefully. Her body is warm. Is she sick, or is it something else?

26

I check my phone as I drive—no missed calls, no text messages, nothing. I feel like getting a coffee. That should renew my body and my mind. I park outside a Starbucks that I visit sometimes. A man is sitting with a large camera and is interviewing two women. A moped is parked on the sidewalk. Two men are smoking and laughing. I enter the store and stand in line behind a weird man who smiles at me. He looks like Albert Einstein. I'm forced to hear his conversation.

"What can I get you?" a young black worker asks him.

"Uh, let me see. Coffee…black," he replies.

"What size, sir? Tall, grande, or Venti," she asks.

"Don't you have small?" he says.

"Well the tall is the small."

"Why don't you call it *small* then?" he says.

He pays with change, which forces me to wait. He seems like a loose cannon, a man with too much time on his hands. He wears grubby boots. There's a bizarre grease on the top. It's funny how you notice things around you when your mind is restless. It's as if I'm an editor on a movie, seeing every detail through a wide-angle lens.

I check my phone again—nothing. It's finally my turn in line.

"Hi, what can I get started for you?" the worker asks.

"Just a coffee, tall."

"Would you like any baked goods?"

"No, thanks."

I pay the bill with a five and put the coins in the tip jar. I meander over to the counter. That weird guy smiles at me again.

"How old is your cat?" he asks.

"What?"

"I see you have a cat."

"I don't have a cat."

"Oh, well, I see your pants have cat hair on them. It looks like a shade of tan. A tabby, I bet."

"It's my sister's cat," I say.

"It was rubbing against you. It's marking you as its territory. I won't go near you now. I don't want to invade the cat's territory."

"I thought the territory thing is just for other cats," I reply, humoring him.

"No. It's for all warm-blooded animals."

"How do you know this?"

"I used to be a vet, before the accident."

"Can I just stand here in silence?" I finally ask.

"I'm sorry," he says.

A coffee machine sounds.

"What's the name?" he asks.

The machine shuts off.

"What?" I shout, filling the place with my voice. A customer reading the newspaper looks up.

"What's your sister's cat's name?"

"I don't know."

"So you got marked by a cat you don't know. That's not good. I love cats, but I can't have any more. My last one was bi-polar," he goes.

"I don't care, sir," I say.

"The cat would smile and be happy. And then as soon as I turned my back, it would growl and hiss at me."

"Tall black coffee," a pimply-faced worker yells.

I reach for the drink.

"Hey, isn't that mine?" the weird guy says.

I put the cup back down. "Go ahead," I say.

"I have another tall black coffee," the same worker yells.

I grab the cup.

"Are you copying me?" the guy says.

I think about adding sugar, but I can't be in this store any longer. I head to the door.

"Nice chatting," the man says.

I drive home sipping the steaming brew. As I walk into my house, the sound of silence subdues me—no video games blasting, no kids fighting, no husband talking. It's a sound that I don't want right now. I hate sitting around. I need to talk to my husband. Is he okay? I have no idea. I need to take action.

I meander into the kitchen and set my purse down on the table. It's too quiet in here. I stare at my phone, pressing a button to light the screen. I take another sip of my coffee and glance through the window into my backyard. A man is sitting in our swing. Is that Michael? No! It's that man in the trench coat from my dream. He turns, the sun reflecting from his bald head. I drop the coffee. It explodes over the counter, burning my arm.

"Shit!"

I look back, but the man is gone. I grab a towel and wipe the coffee from my arm. A knock at the door echoes throughout the house. I stop cold. I can't breathe. I'm suffocating! Should I answer it? What if it's that man?

I creep through the kitchen to the entryway. A figure is outside the stained-glass window. Who is it? Maybe it's Michael. Or maybe it's the other guy. As I move closer toward the white door, I hear giggling. It's the sound not from an adult, but from kids. I take a breath and open the door. Sophia, Ben, and Jimmy run in. Joyce's familiar smile greets me.

"I want to be first player!" Ben yells.

"No! I do!" Sophie counters.

"No! Me!" Jimmy says.

Joyce enters and sees the coffee stain on my blouse and my arm. "What happened?" she asks.

"I just spilled some coffee. I'm fine."

"It's all over you. Be careful... Any luck?"

"No, let me check again."

I check my phone, which is still in my hand. I hold the number to speed dial Michael. I don't get a ring.

"Hello this is Michael, sorry that—"

I shake my head again, just as I have done four times today.

"Maybe he's having trouble with his phone? When was the last time you talked to him?" she asks.

"Yesterday evening my time. After dinner. But he abruptly ended the call."

"Do you have the number for any of his colleagues?"

"Well, he's there with two from marketing, but I don't have their numbers."

"Can you call the main office?" she asks.

Joyce suggests things that I've already considered. She possesses wisdom and street smarts, just as she always has over the years. I can remember her advice with guys in high school. In fact, I can recall her helping me with my first period, as I was too embarrassed to talk to Mom. But what she lacks in this situation is that special feeling, that special instinct that only married couples share after taking the vow of marriage. It's a feeling that radiates from your heart to your brain. It's always there, even when you're sleeping.

"Something just doesn't feel right," I say.

"Well, what are you going to do?" she asks.

I look into the eyes of my sister. I tell her what I'm going to do not with words, but with my eyes. While couples possess a special instinct at marriage, sisters possess a special bond that is present from birth. Joyce knows what I'm going to do.

27

I stab the rabbit and take a bite out of it.

"How is the meal, *mademoiselle*?" the server asks.

"Very good," I say.

"And you, *monsieur*?"

"Wonderful," Michael replies.

"*Exceptionnel*. Please let me know if I can be of assistance."

Michael and I are sitting inside the Eiffel Tower with a view of the Bellagio Fountains. We didn't even have dinner reservations, but Michael's hundred-dollar handshake put us on the list. We had taken the elevator up and walked through the restless crowd to our table. I feel like a million dollars next to him. He knows how to please a woman. Does he do this for his wife? Does it really matter? I'm here and she is not.

I've never had rabbit before. Its taste is similar to chicken, yet its texture is chewier. Michael played it safe with steak, but the night is far from over. I look at him slice his meat, stab the piece with his fork, and chew on it. He moves his lips when he chews. He must really like his meat. I can't stop looking at him. I feel bad for Michael. He has been different, more fun, and deeper than the others have been. Does he know? If he knows, then why hasn't he done something about it? I've been on edge ever since this morning. My heart has been beating faster. I feel sweatier, dirtier. I'm afraid of what's to come. A part of me wants this moment to last forever. Michael has filled a void inside of me, present since that night five years ago. But I can't trust happiness anymore. Tragedy is everywhere. It stabs you when you least expect it, just as it had that night.

"You must really like that rabbit," Michael says.

"When in Paris…" I say.

"Your plate is so ironic."

"What do you mean?"

"Well, they serve you rabbit with steamed carrots. Don't you see the irony?" Michael says.

"Because a rabbit eats carrots?"

"Yeah. They put the carrots right there in front of the rabbit. It's as if the chef is taunting him. Like the only time he gets fresh, cooked carrots is when he's dead."

Michael makes me laugh. He's so cute when he's geeky. I take a bite of rabbit, and then a bite of carrot.

"And they meet again in my belly," I say.

He laughs.

Michael and I watch another show at the Bellagio. A black man with a camera offers to take our picture. Michael looks at me as if he wants to pose. While he is cute, he is so naive.

After I finish eating, I pull out a cigarette.

"Do you have a light?" I ask Michael.

He roots around in his coat.

"Here we go," he says.

He strikes the match and offers me the flame. Michael is such a nice little boy. I inhale a deep puff, filling my lungs with tobacco.

"*Madame*, I am sorry. There is no smoking in here," the server says.

I sneak one last puff, and then kill the cigarette on my plate.

After dinner, Michael and I find our way back to the car.

"So, what else do you want to do?" he asks in the parking garage.

"That's a loaded question."

"It's only ten o'clock," he says.

"The night is young. Let's take a walk."

"Where?" he asks.

"Everywhere."

"How about the Stratosphere?"

"Sure."

As we drive, the air seems cooler, but maybe that's because I'm sweating. I know what I have to do, what I have planned to do for months. But I can't believe the time is here. I feel like a high school girl again moments before my first time. I remember closing the store at the mall where I had worked with that jock two years older than me. I was rebelling, and he was cute. I remember him joking with me about virginity, and the look that he gave me when I had given him the green light. I remember driving in his car, a convertible. I was so anxious, as I knew that I would experience something that I had questioned for years. I hope the deed that I'm about to do doesn't end as that night had ended—covered in blood.

We park at the Stratosphere. I let Michael lead the way. Signs are plastered everywhere for the vampire show "Bite." How fitting.

After using the ladies' room, we exit the Stratosphere. The night air hits us. Valet drivers shuffle. Drunks exit a cab. Tourists march. The lights from the Strip radiate. A couple exits a limo; the man is wearing a tuxedo. He looks handsome.

This is it. I can feel it. It's now or never. My heart races. A crowd wanders in front of us. I steer Michael away from the people. The sound of screaming is in the air. It must be the rides on top of the Stratosphere. We turn the corner and amble down a secluded sidewalk. I am so nervous. Get a grip. I can do this. I know I can. Just breathe.

Michael keeps clearing his throat. Is he nervous too?

Suddenly, I see lights that look familiar. As my eyes adjust, I realize they're the lights from a wedding chapel—the chapel where I had been married. What am I doing here? I can't do this. But I must. I need a cigarette.

28

Her hand is so clammy. She keeps kneading my arm. Is she nervous? Is she going to miss me? Tomorrow I'll be on a plane headed back to the Northeast. I can't wait to see Melissa. I will use this energy to foster our marriage, to enhance it, to make it grow stronger…at least I hope I will.

We exit the Stratosphere; the dry desert air encircles us. It's refreshing to be this warm outside after the sun goes down. Valet drivers move around like chess pieces. College guys hoot and holler as they exit a cab. Tourists are everywhere. I love the lights from the Strip. A limo stops. A couple exits; the woman is breathtaking in her white gown.

Rachel and I walk toward the action, but then she guides me down another way. The faint sound of screaming hits me. Who would be screaming? But then, I remember all the posters for the rides above us. I feel so anxious. I don't want this night, this trip, to end. How are we going to part ways? Should I give her my cell number? No. I don't want to get caught. How about I get her email address? But then I might be tempted to keep a relationship on the side. No, this has to end tonight; it *must* end. I'm so nervous. Should I end this now? But we still have some time left. I want to explore a little more. I see wedding chapels lining Las Vegas Boulevard. Rachel's squeeze suddenly gets tighter. What is going through her mind right now? As I try to decide what to say, she lights a cigarette.

"I don't remember you smoking so much," I say.

She had a cigarette for the first time after dinner tonight. Wait… Wasn't she smoking when we first met? How quickly I forgot. Perhaps that's a good thing.

"There's a lot about me that you don't know," she replies.

"I had fun today," I say.

"Well the day's not over yet."

"There's probably a mountain of messages waiting for me."

"They'll forgive you. Remember, it's Vegas."

"I fly home tomorrow night. How will this end?"

"What happens in Vegas…" she begins.

"…stays in Vegas. I know, but will we keep in touch? *Can* we keep in touch?"

I'm talking too much. She stops walking and attacks me with a kiss. I can taste the cigarette. I have never kissed a smoker before. Her voraciousness puts my mind at ease. I should just relax. Lust can't be pondered.

"Let's take this to your convention booth," she whispers.

"Why? It's late. What if someone sees us?" I say.

"You have a convention key. Live a little. I wanna do it in the C.E.O.'s office."

My toes curl inside my shoes. I can't believe she wants to go back to the convention. I'm terrified, yet excited beyond my wits. This woman, this creature, never fails to stop amazing me. Just when I think it's over, it's just beginning.

"You're going to be the end of me," I say.

She drops the cigarette and steps on it with her heel. We head back to my car. She pets my leg as I drive, my cock bulging out of my slacks. I am so horny.

The Hilton is in front of us. If I park there, it's a long walk to the convention center. I should just park in front of it. I have a VIP pass that I have never even used.

"Let's park in front," I say.

"The closer the better."

I roll up to the parking gate manned by an attendant. He looks about 20 from my angle, probably a college kid.

"Good evening, sir. You're going the wrong way," he jokes.

"I just forgot something," I lie, flashing my parking badge.

"No problem," he says, raising the gate and waving us in.

I enter the deserted lot. I get to park right in front.

"What did you forget?" Rachel asks.

"You tell me."

I park my rental and place the parking pass on the dash. I put my convention badge around my neck, and then help Rachel out, holding her purse until she stands up. We behold the ominous building. Only a few people scatter the area. The place looks bigger at night, more enigmatic, a fortress after a plague, or maybe a prison. I near the main entrance; the opaque doors are all shut. What am I doing? Is it okay to go inside?

"They might be closed," I say.

"Vegas never closes."

JONATHAN STURAK

I reach the doors. I try the first one, but it's locked. I try another one, and another, but they're all locked. I feel like an imposter, a magician who lost his Vegas act.

The last door opens. A beefy security officer in a yellow shirt sizes me up. He remains mute, which startles me.

"Hi. I have a booth on the floor. I forgot my briefcase," I chuckle.

He wears a stone face. Only his eyes move from me to Rachel. Does he know the real reason I am here—to bring this escort inside and fuck her brains out in the back of my booth? If he knows, would he tell me?

"Badge?" he says.

I show him my booth badge. It seems to do the trick; he holds the door for me. But perhaps Rachel is the reason he allows us in. He could just want to watch her ass sway as she saunters inside.

Only half of the lights are illuminated. The place looks even more like an airplane hangar. There are no humans scurrying, no chatter swirling, no life flowing. It's a maze of booths. We turn down aisle C. A shadow shifts up ahead. I stop. Rachel looks at me with strange eyes. What's going on? I'm a mouse in a maze. As my eyes adjust to the movement, I see a janitor pushing a broom.

Rachel giggles. "Don't be so jumpy, Mister Harris."

"Someone's going to find us."

"Shh…"

We keep going. I've passed these booths probably 10 times since arriving, yet they all look different without people around. I have to use the booth numbers as a guide just to find my own. I see "13-C."

"Wait, we've passed it," I say.

"Ha, you're lost, huh?"

140

I turn around and see my abandoned booth. The computers are off. The lights are dead. The trinkets are packed up. I read my company's name under my breath to make sure it's my booth. "Bio Algorithms."

Rachel darts inside laughing like a kid going skinny-dipping.

"Wait," I say.

"What's back here?" she asks.

I give her a taste of her own medicine. I go to her, pull down her blouse, exposing her shoulders, and then kiss her skin. She tastes salty. I kiss her neck; her skin is warm. She chuckles. My pointed cock hurts, my tight pants bending it. I rub my fingers over her arms, and then grab her breasts. They feel so soft hidden inside her top. I want her now more than anything.

She laughs, this time louder. I move up and press her lips against mine. I kiss her with force, the way a man only kisses his mistress. She mumbles something between my attacks. I try to detect it not with my ears, but with my mouth's sense of touch. I push her against the back table. Keychains fall onto the floor, but I don't care. She pulls back just enough to verbalize her words.

"Come on, save some energy…"

What does she mean? I thought she wants this here, now. I pounce on her. She laughs again.

"…save some energy for your journey."

"Journey?" I say.

I go back to her neck. I don't care what she is saying. My penis is throbbing. I bring her closer and reach under her shirt. As I kiss her neck, I feel a pain in my chest. It's not a dull ache, but rather a sharp, piercing twinge. It's right over my heart. Suddenly, it jabs me, pummeling my pain receptors. As I stand frozen, it hits me hard. I know what it is now. The creature that I'm holding in my arms is not a woman, but rather a slippery snake that has just shown its fangs.

"Back," she says in a deeper, rawer voice.

I move slowly, carefully, my mind not yet caught up to my body. As I break our embrace, I suddenly feel cold and alone. My erection fades, the blood now rushing to my brain. Where am I?

When I move three steps back, I see the tempting temptress clutching a tiny pistol. She doesn't shake, doesn't move. Her eyes burn into me like hot coals. I've never had a gun pointed at me before. It feels like a million eyes are glaring at my soul. There's nowhere to turn, nowhere to go. And once the eyes blink, they will capture my life.

"What are you doing?" I ask.

"Sorry, dear. This is strictly business. Now open that door," she says.

I feel not like a magician, but a member of the audience in awe of the featured act. A million questions run through my mind, but a piece of me still craves her, still wants to bend her over and fuck her silly. Perhaps this is all part of a bizarre fantasy of hers.

"Move!" she yells.

She is serious, dead serious. I can't ask questions. I can only listen to her—the woman with the gun.

"Where?" I ask.

She points with the gun toward the back door. I place my hand on the combination lock. It feels hot, but that's probably because I'm cold. I can sense the gun, the million eyes, staring at me. I fumble with the lock, the neurons in my brain failing to fire.

"Come on," she says.

I take a breath. I can do this. Forget the creature behind me. Just enter the code as if it's a normal day.

I try again and somehow get it right. The door opens, breaking the first layer of defense. Shadows fill the confined space. I enter the coffin as the stale air strangles me.

"What is it you want?" I ask.

"You know what I want."

"I can give you money."

"Not as much as your little computer program is going to get me. Get it open!"

What is happening!? Should I yell? What do I do? I need to get out of here. Will that security guard hear me if I scream?

"Safe! Now!" she says.

Enough thinking. I go to the safe. I take it slow, dead slow. After a few concise twists, the second layer of security is breached. The silver case breathes the musty air.

"Now put it over there," she instructs.

I put the case on a side table.

"Open it."

I spin the intricate dial and press the lock, the click echoes inside the room and filters through my nerves. Then, I open the case, the third layer. I look at the laptop and then at the face of Rachel. Her lips form a smile that I have never seen before, but then again, there is a lot about her that I haven't seen.

She grabs a Bio Algorithms bag from the side. "In the bag."

What can I do? What can I say? Is there any way out of this?

I put the laptop in the bag. "It's useless without my smart card," I say.

"My next request. I'll take that too."

She gestures with the gun. I hold my wallet out. She's chipping away at the security checks, but there are still two left, two important ones.

"The smart card doesn't even matter, you need my finger-print."

"Sweetie, I already got that," she laughs.

What does she mean? I look at my 10 fingers. While they are trembling, they are still intact. But then, I remember that first morning that I had awoken to an empty room with strange grease on my finger. It's all adding up. But there is still one more level of security that has been tested for decades.

"Just try cracking my password," I say.

"It's called a Brute Force Algorithm. I'm sure the North Koreans can figure it out, don't you?"

She's right again. I have underestimated this female specimen. All these layers of security are useless against the human factor. What's the point of locks, codes, and fingerprints when a human can be held at gunpoint to open the safe? Who the hell is she!?

"Brute Force Algorithm. I thought you didn't know—"

"There's a lot you don't know about me. Now put it in the bag!"

I drop my wallet inside.

"Empty your pockets too!"

I comply, putting my cell phone in with my other items, but there is something inside my pocket that I don't remove, something that is irreplaceable.

Rachel sets the bag down and uses her free hand to check my pants. She pats my left pocket and grazes my groin, chuckling. Then, she feels my right pocket and finds the item that stops my heart.

"Everything!" she yells.

I waver. She forces the gun into my chest. These other items don't hit me as hard as the one that she demands. It's the smallest one, weighing less than an ounce, but it is the heaviest. I reach inside my pocket and search for something, anything, other than this item. I hope to find a knife or a pistol, but these things are not there, only the item that I remove—my wedding ring.

"You won't be needing this anymore," she says, snatching it.

I remove my Rolex watch. Perhaps she will trade me.

"Ahh, save it. Time is the only thing you have left. Now, clean this up!"

I close the case and lock it back inside the safe. The place looks clean, just as it was when I had entered, but there is something missing, something that may never be replaced.

"Now let's go!"

"Where?"

"I'm taking you someplace special," she says.

Rachel exits the back room first, holding the bag in one hand, the pistol in the other. I lock the door and look at her for direction. She gestures toward the exit. I move into the dark aisle. I can hear my breathing. It's fast, erratic. I'm sick to my stomach as if I had eaten something sour, something mean, even more intense than octopus.

Rachel follows a few steps behind. Even though we walk on carpet, I can hear her heels stabbing the floor. As we turn down another aisle, I hear someone whistling. In the distance, the same janitor is sweeping the concrete. I want to yell to grab his attention. But what will Rachel do? Will she shoot? Or will she vacillate? Does she have it in her to kill? Will I feel the million eyes pierce my back when she pulls the trigger? I can't read her anymore. Before I can react, Rachel reacts for me.

"Come here," she whispers.

She grabs me, digging the barrel into my gut. As the janitor nears, she smothers me with her lips. She tastes bitter like an orange left in the sun. I try not to kiss her, but she finds her way into my mouth with her tongue. Is she enjoying this?

"Only in Vegas," I hear from the janitor as he detours past us.

Rachel digs the gun deeper into my gut. "Come on, you horny boy."

145

We move to the door. I dart my eyes in all directions, but see no one. Where is that security guard? I open the door. Rachel holds on to me. My senses focus on the gun pressed against my side. We walk through the deserted parking lot, the sound of her heels beating like a heart, steady, hypnotic. They sound nothing like the rhythm of my heart.

"Okay. You drive. Keep it cool," she says.

"Tell me where we're going?"

"You'll find out soon enough."

"Listen, I'm not getting in that car unless you tell me where we're going."

"You're in no position to make demands. This is called a gun. And it's a big bargaining chip."

I detest this woman. I wish I could grab her neck and smash her face against my car, or take off her heel and impale her heart. But I'm in a tough position to do anything other than listen. I enter the car. As she scurries around, her eyes puncture me. Rachel steps inside and positions the gun behind her purse.

"Drive," she says.

I pull out. My senses are heightened. Every clunk of the shifter, turn of the steering wheel, or roll of the car sends shivers through my spine. We roll up to the parking attendant. I lock eyes with him for a moment. I wish I could tell him that I am in danger. I channel all of my energy, all of my rage, into my eyes. He sits up. Does he know? But then, he just smiles and waves us through.

The drive is slow. We take Las Vegas Boulevard south. It's so quiet inside my casket. The lights surround me, bounce off my face, and tickle my eyes. We stop at a traffic light next to the Monte Carlo. Hundreds of people walk across the street. A man dances. A mother pushes a stroller. Three sexy women stomp. There is life all around me, yet I feel dead.

I drive past the Mandalay Bay. I glance in the rear-view mirror and see the trailing lights.

"Where are we going?" I ask again.

"You're too impatient, just like when you fuck."

I cringe at the fact that I had my dick inside her, surrounded by her slippery flesh that milked me. At the same time, I wish I had been deep enough to see the monster within.

I see the back of the Las Vegas sign. I read the message in my mind, "Drive Carefully – Come Back Soon." It should read, "Come Back Alive." Tourists gather around the front. A man with a camera takes a picture of a young woman with brunette hair.

We drive for nearly a half hour, my breathing slows, yet my heart rate increases. I listen to Rachel's simple directions—"left here" or "right at the next intersection." As the miles rack up, the lights get darker until there are no more lights. We are in the void of the desert, a place where light fails to exist. The only signal of life is the macadam road created by humans.

"Turn off here," she says.

"There's no road."

There is desert sand on our sides. Is she serious? I look over at her. I haven't seen her face since we've left the Strip, but what I witness scares me—her red lips forming a smirk that I have never seen before.

"I'm glad you got the navigation system for my trip back. Told you it was important," she says.

All along this lonely drive I thought she was taking me somewhere that she knew, somewhere with a possible way out. But all she was really doing was escaping the lights.

I turn off onto the sandy gravel. The tires crunch, a sound that terrifies me for another 20 minutes.

"This should be fine. Stop here."

I press the brake. I see the bright red brake lights in the rearview. Is she going to kill me?

"You said you wanted to go to the desert. Well, here we are. Come on, baby, admit it, it was fun while it lasted."

Her words make my breathing stop. I feel robbed, cheated at the most deadly game in Vegas—the game of life. The good time I had was with someone else. This woman, this monster, is someone far different from the creature I had met.

She looks outside, and then I get it. She is not going to kill me with the gun, but rather let the desert do it.

"Get out," she says.

"What?"

"What part of *get out* don't you understand?"

I open the door. Dust enters the car and attacks my face. I want to cough, but I can't.

"Maybe you'll find another horny traveler out here," she says.

I step out. The cool desert air surrounds me. My eyes see nothing but the light from inside the car, the only light left for miles and miles. Rachel slides over to the driver's seat. She presses the button to lower the convertible top, keeping the gun on me. Once the convertible motor stops, the venomous vixen looks at me with her hungry eyes.

"All you boys think with your dicks!"

She sets the gun on the passenger seat. I have a moment, the last moment, to make a move. But as I lunge at her, the car launches forward, dust and gravel flying into the air.

"Hey! Wait!" I yell, banging the trunk.

It's too late. I can only watch the red tail lights trail into the night. I follow them, the only thing to follow, but the void of the desert quickly consumes them.

I am now alone. I see black. I smell nothing. I hear no one. I can only taste the grit of the earth in my teeth.

"Hello!?" I yell.

Nothing returns, not even an echo. All I hear is the last sound I want to hear—the sound of silence. Is this death? Perhaps she has already shot me. How would I know? Maybe I'm in hell.

29

The convention building towers over us. I hold on to Michael's arm as he leads me through the parking lot.

"They might be closed," Michael says.

"Vegas never closes."

I am so nervous. My hands are sweaty. I wonder if Michael knows. Can he feel my arm twitching? He thinks we are going to fuck in his convention booth. Maybe I should let him have some fun first before I reveal my true colors. But he's already had too much fun. *I've* already had too much fun. I need to get down to business. There is no time for fooling around. This is my only chance to make it work. I need to break through several tough layers of security.

A security officer stops us at the door, but Michael tries to play it cool. I can tell he is nervous. He always adds a little chuckle at the end of his words when he's nervous. I'm sure the security officer doesn't sense it, but I can. It's Michael's tell.

We enter the structure. Only half the lights are shining. Michael looks like he doesn't even know where his booth is. I hold on to him as we see a janitor sweeping. Michael is so jumpy. I giggle as a way to calm him, and to calm myself. Just be cool. Stick to the plan. I can do this. This is just a job.

Michael leads me past his booth. I let him try to get his bearings. Then, he leads me to it—Bio Algorithms. It's dark, which is good. I see the room in the back, the room that I had planned to breach for months. I run in the back and snicker. I toy with Michael like a schoolgirl in her date's basement. He puts his arms around me. I clutch my purse and spin, letting him have his way. Michael grabs my blouse, and then kisses my shoulders. His tongue is cold as he licks and smacks. He runs his hands across my body as if I'm a piece of meat. Wow. He is really horny. Through our clothes, his erect cock prods my clit. I get wet instantly. Should I let him have it? What to do? What to do?

Michael grabs my breasts with force. I open my purse as I use words to play with him. I have to do this now. As he increases his vigor, I grab the cold metal object that I carried around all night, the object that I thought about when I stabbed my rabbit over dinner, the object that I checked in the ladies' room at the Stratosphere. I clutch the pistol as I have a dozen times before and jab it into his chest, into his heart. I transform into the creature that lay dormant inside of me.

"Back," I say in a deeper, rawer voice.

He breaks our embrace. I stare at him with the eyes of the creature. His brow furrows. He looks shocked. I can tell his mind is racing, filling with questions faster than a fire filling a building.

I hold the gun firmly. I cannot go back to the woman I once was just moments ago. I have already made my bed.

"What are you doing?" he asks.

"Sorry, dear. This is strictly business. Now open that door," I say.

Michael hesitates.

"Move!" I yell.

He jumps to action. I have to let him know that I mean business. I am not the same person. I have to make his mind recognize that. It's all business now. Michael finally gets the door unlocked. I glance around and see the safe. I instruct him to open it. He knows what I want. I watch him work like the mail boy on his first day. I keep an ear out for any trouble, but I know that we are all alone inside this coffin. He finally opens the safe. There it is— the laptop that I have dreamed about.

I find a Bio Algorithms bag. Michael puts the laptop inside. He tries to reason with me, but I know a thing or two about computers. After all, my love was also a computer scientist.

I strip Michael of his wallet and his phone. And then, I want the item that he thinks I don't know about. I felt it during dinner when I caressed his leg. I take his ring, his marriage, his wife, and his life and throw them in the trash. Michael did this to himself.

I tell him to leave. We walk through the convention hall. I carry the bag in one hand, and hold the gun against him with the other. As we turn the corner, a shadow is approaching. It's that janitor. I hesitate for a moment, but then use an old trick to evade detection. I spin Michael, dig the gun into his gut, and then kiss him. I give it my Academy Award performance, licking, kissing, sucking. The janitor has no idea what he is witnessing.

We make it out of the convention and back into the rental car. The night air feels refreshing against my sweaty skin. I direct Michael as he drives past the parking attendant.

The convention center grows smaller in the side-view mirror. It all went smoother than I had expected. I got in, breached the layers of security, and then got out without a scratch. Michael detests me, but that's okay. I had fun with him while it lasted.

The Strip is alive. People surround us. Lights bathe us. Energy flows. I watch Michael as he drives. He swallows a lot. He doesn't say anything; he just stares straight at the road in front of him. What is he thinking? I wish I could look into his mind.

We near the Vegas sign. I read the message silently, "Drive Carefully – Come Back Soon." The sign should say, "Come Back Rich."

We continue toward the unknown, passing a huge toy building called "South Point." I wonder if he thinks I'm going to kill him and dump his body in the desert. I already got what I had come to get. I don't need to kill *another* man. I'll let the desert do that.

The radiance trails in the side-view mirror. I instruct Michael to drive farther and farther away from the light. I don't know where we are going exactly, but I will know when we get there.

After driving on the interstate for at least 20 miles of desert, I tell Michael to turn off the road. This looks like a spot that not even an animal would call home. It feels like a void in outer space, a place where life has not found a way to survive. I lead Michael farther into the sandy desert, miles and miles. I keep going until my gut tells me this is the end.

I instruct Michael to stop. He freaks out, horror filling his eyes. I kick him out and give him some lasting words as I lower the convertible top. As I speed away, I hear him yelling from behind and pounding on the rental car. But just as fast, I hear nothing.

After about five minutes, I stop the car in the middle of the desert. The engine idles. The smell of sand swirls. The color black surrounds me. I feel alone, lost. I get a sense of Michael's problem. How long will he live before the desert consumes him? While he is alone, I am not. I turn to my companion—the navigation system.

The device says that the closest landmark is Jean, Nevada. I check the built-in destinations and select the Las Vegas sign. I know where to go from there.

"Drive 22 miles," the female voice instructs.

I let the system guide me. I think I've confused it by driving in the desert, but it still works. I wonder what the computer inside the GPS thinks. Does it know that I have just dumped a man in the desert? Would it care? I stop thinking and let the device guide me back to the road, back to civilization.

As I reach the interstate, my cell phone rings.

"Yeah," I say.

All I can hear is wind.

"What!?" I yell.

Again, I can't hear.

"Let me pull over."

I get off at the first exit and pull into a gas station. The Strip shines in the distance.

"Sorry. I'm here now," I say.

"What happened?" the male voice asks.

"It's done."

"Excellent. Where are you now?"

"Just driving back in."

"Where did you dump the body?"

"I left him in the desert."

"*Left him*? Hopefully you left him with two lead bullets in his brain."

"No, I just dumped him out."

"I told you to dispose of him! I trusted you on this one."

"He's never going to survive out there alone. If the coyotes don't get him, the heat tomorrow will."

"Listen, bitch. If you fucked this up and I get—"

"I got it taken care of!" I shout.

"Just get back here. I need some time to get things sorted out."

I hang up the phone. My breathing picks up. The tears come on. Why do I keep letting him rule me? I loathe him. This is the last time I do this.

I grab a cigarette from my bag and light it up. I suck in the tobacco and let it swirl in my lungs. As I try to calm down, I lift the Bio Algorithms bag onto the seat. His wallet falls out. A picture of Michael's family drops. Michael looks happy in the picture holding his smiling kids. His wife beams next to him.

The Strip is in front of me. From my perspective, it looks so small, so insignificant.

30

There are two hundred people sitting in the pews. The smell of roses surrounds me. I fix my wedding dress. My heart is racing. Michael is at the altar. Everyone chatters. There is Mom up front. There's Tracy from my high school cheerleading days. This dress is too tight. I feel fat. I shouldn't have eaten that sandwich. I'm going to throw up. That would look *great*, throwing up on my wedding day. I can't believe this is happening. Is Michael really the one for me, the one forever?

"Are you ready, dear?" my father asks.

He scoops me up in his arms. Aww, my dad. He's still alive. He looks healthy with his full head of hair, even though it's getting gray.

The music starts. The crowd silences. This is it. My dad starts the walk.

"Just like in rehearsal," I whisper to myself.

I walk in step with Dad. My aunt takes a picture. My uncle smiles. I pass a woman in red heels on Michael's side. She stares at me as if she has a million eyes. Who is she? I feel safe on my dad's arm. I focus on Michael up ahead. He has his back to me. Why isn't he looking at me?

We near the altar. Mom is crying. Don't cry, Mom. I near Michael. His suit is ruffled. He stares forward, faceless. There is Joyce standing with the other bridesmaids. There is Michael's cousin as the best man. Suddenly, my dad moves his arm. I don't want him to let me go. Please, Dad, stay by my side.

And then like that, he lets me go.

I am alone now. Where is the priest? I move next to Michael. He seems taller. Why doesn't he look at me? Should I call his name? I can feel the eyes of the crowd burning into me. I want to run. I want to be alone. As I near Michael, I smell cologne that I have never smelled before. This is not Michael. Who is it? I'm standing next to him, yet I still can't see his face. He has an Ohio State pin on his suit. Michael didn't go to Ohio State.

"Michael," I mutter.

As I hold my breath, Michael turns. It's not him! It's the evil creature with the shaved head! His eyes flare. I stop breathing and look around. By my side, I see the evil man cloned ten times. I whip around to my dad, but he too is a duplicate. I face the crowd as hundreds of clones glare at me. The room spins. I'm trapped. I see a man approaching us. It's the priest wearing black.

"Father, help me!"

His face comes into focus. He too is the evil man.

"Please fasten your seatbelt," the priest says.

What does he mean?

"Ma'am, please fasten your seatbelt," he says again.

Suddenly, a burst of light hits my eyes. I jar awake on an airplane. A male flight attendant is standing over me.

"Sorry for waking you, but the captain has asked that you fasten your seatbelt," he says.

I grip my belt as he leaves me. I try to catch my breath. My mind aches. There's a group of college-aged guys in front of me wearing a "Las Vegas or Bust" T-shirt. They are standing and laughing. A middle-aged woman wearing sunglasses skulks past me, a look of sorrow molded in her lips. Through the window, the sun burns in the blue sky. Down below, I can barely make out flat farmland.

The flight attendant walks by.

"Where are we?" I ask him.

"I think we're over Kansas."

I am halfway there, halfway to the desert, halfway to the place that houses my husband. I feel good for taking action, but I'm terrified to find what lies below.

31

I need to find a way out of the scorching sun. The feeling is beyond a feeling. My white shirt is no longer white; dust and sweat now consume the fibers. I look around and see only the color brown. I keep moving, but I have no energy. My shoes are dragging in the sand. I need water—even just another drop. I would trade my finger for a drop of water. I can live without a finger. I would even give my left ring finger. There's no ring there anymore; there will never be again.

My lips are crusty. I can't even cry anymore. I keep moving. The sun is at its highest spot. I don't know how much longer I can move. In the distance, there's something black lying on the ground. I shuffle toward it, my eyes trying to focus.

"Shit," I say as I recognize the item.

My black suit coat is in the sand. My badge lies next to it in its grave. I just walked in circles for hours. I laugh uncontrollably. Why is this funny? There is the small cactus that I killed. This is like some bizarre game. Perhaps, I'm dreaming, or even worse, perhaps I'm dead.

I try to swallow, but I have no more saliva. I wonder how much longer I will live, maybe a few hours, maybe less. How much more can my body take? I wish there were a way out. As I stand here recognizing my circle, I see something moving in the vast desert. I blink, and it still looks like it's there. It looks human. It's a person.

"Hey!" I scream.

I move toward the body that's just standing there. It must be 50 yards away.

"Over here!" I yell.

I pick up my steps. It looks like a woman. She sees me. As I get closer, I recognize the black woman that I've seen before. She has the African black skin that is impenetrable by the sun. What is she doing out here? She's naked. Her bare breasts are exposed. She's holding something. It's a baby. She's breastfeeding a baby. What the fuck?

"Help me!" I shout.

I near her, cutting the distance. I'm 10 yards away, but suddenly I trip. I go down, hard, and roll in the sand. I see the sun. My head spins. I sit up and look for her, but all that's there is the infinite desert. Where did she go? Wait… There she is some 200 yards away. How did she get there so fast?

I continue toward the woman, toward something. How did I end up out here? Why did I end up out here? I am a good person. I pay my bills. I wash my car by hand. I go to church on holidays. I protect my family. I want to cry at the thought of Ben, Sophia, and Melissa, but I have no tears left. I don't deserve to be out here.

"I am so sorry, God. I know I've made many mistakes. Please don't let me die, not like this," I say aloud.

Las Vegas is a forbidden city. It is the place where sin flourishes and lights can quickly turn to shadows. I got caught up in the city.

As I near the woman, she flies into the air. I can barely see her. She squawks above me. She's that bird, and she is still waiting for me to die. She's been following me for hours. She must be hungry. I tumble again, this time my right ankle twists. I rub my face. It's like sandpaper. My hair is like straw. I put my hands in my armpits. There's still an ounce of sweat. I run my fingers over it and taste it. It's salty, foul, but it's liquid.

As I lie here in the sand, I stare at the sky. My mind is numb. I can't think straight. I don't even know who I am. I am just a speck of sand in the world's sandbox.

Marriage is so fragile. It's a ticking time bomb ready to explode. Sure we buy into the idea of happiness, of undeniable love shared between two individuals who vowed to depart only in death. But the love held together by marriage can explode at any time—a jealous wife catching her husband, a husband losing his wife to drugs, a past fling splitting apart spouses. These scenarios lurk around every corner; they can happen any day, any hour, any minute; they can happen anywhere. Marriage is so hard; it takes so much to make it work. Beyond the darkness that stalks marriages, there is only one true love in this universe, one love that can never be broken, one love that only a mother possesses with her child. A mother is stronger than jealousy, stronger than drugs, stronger than a past fling. A mother will always be there for her child. As the sun singes me, burning out my eyes, burning out my brain, I wonder where my mother is right now.

As the cloudless sky fills my eyes, I hold my breath. I want to die now. I am ready. It's over. Seconds pass. My lungs scream. Just a little longer and I will be gone. But then, my body forces me to suck air. I gasp uncontrollably. I need a pillow to do this. I grab sand and pour it into my nose and mouth. I hold my breath again. As I count the seconds, I see something in the sky. It's not that woman flying around, but something higher, something up in the light. I know what it is. I've seen it before. It's another airplane, another symbol from above.

"Follow the plane," a voice whispers.

I know where to go now, where to exhaust my remaining energy. I must try. I cough out the sand. I suddenly feel renewed. Instead of barking at the sun, instead of taunting it, instead of hiding from it, use it against itself. I look at the plane and mark its direction with the sun.

32

The vast desert is below me. Is there any life down there? My back aches. This seat is so uncomfortable. I feel like I'm in a coffin. How much longer do we have?

"This is the captain speaking. We are making our final descent into Las Vegas."

The drunks in front of me hoot.

"Please ensure all electronic devices are turned off and stowed. We ask that you make sure your tray table is in its upright position and all carry-on luggage is secured under your seats or in an overhead bin. It looks like we have clear skies, temperatures right at a hundred and three on the ground. We will be in Las Vegas soon."

More cheers erupt from the crowd. Everyone seems happy, full of energy. Even the old man next to me looks out of the window. But I am terrified. What will I find on the ground? Where will I begin to look for Michael? Should I start at the convention or his hotel? Should I go to the police?

This time alone has made me think about my marriage, my family, and my life. My wedding day seems like it was just yesterday, but 10 years have passed, 10 years that include owning my first house, losing my father, birthing two children, and being in love. I always trust Michael to be there for me, to provide for his family, and to be honest. I know Michael. I know that he leaves his coffee cups upside down in the sink. I know that he always lays a clean towel on the counter for me when I'm in the shower. I know that he likes his back kneaded when we make love. Whatever happened to Michael must be something beyond his control. He is so smart and educated. He can deduce his way out of any problem. But the desert may have thrown him a curveball. I hope that Michael can see past the lights.

After a rocky descent, we finally touch down. I see the black pyramid through my window. I feel strange being here. There's only one person out here I can rely on, can confide in with my secrets. But that person is missing, and until I find him, I am all alone. Right now, I'm a mess. I haven't looked at my hair since Joyce brought me to the airport.

As I watch the drunks shuffle off, I see that same woman with sunglasses about 10 rows back. She still looks forlorn, a frown frozen on her face. I wonder what brings her here. Perhaps, for similar reasons as me.

Walking from the gate, slot machines fill my view.

"Welcome to Vegas," I mutter.

A man with a single rose runs to that woman. She jumps into the man's arms and kisses him, her frown gone, now transferred to my face.

I brought a carry-on filled with only the essential items. Michael is supposed to come home this evening. I plan to be on that flight with him, but a plan is only worth its weight if it works.

I walk outside. The heat hits me. It turns my skin into sandpaper. But I don't care. I grab a taxi. The driver asks me where I want to go. That question has been rolling around in my mind for hours. I don't know the answer, but I need to respond with a destination. I want to tell him to take me to Michael, but I doubt this grubby guy would know where to go. I figure that I should start at the place where Michael should be, the reason he had come here—the convention center.

It's just after 3:00 in the afternoon. The sun covers the Strip as we drive behind it. I see the Luxor, the buildings of New York-New York, the "PH" of Planet Hollywood. College guys walk with beers in their hands and girls in their eyes. Helicopters whirl around. Cars flow. People stride. All this happens even though we are behind the Strip. Life is everywhere, yet I feel lifeless.

The convention center towers in front of me. The cab driver drops me in front. Several men are wheeling out a plasma TV. A woman is pushing a cart with boxes. I go to the door and slip in next to a group of Asian men in suits. I make my way toward the main hall, but two 20-something women in red shirts are standing guard. They check the badges of three men walking in. What do I say? Do I tell them that I'm looking for my husband? I wish I could plug a cable into their brains to let them know the situation, to let them know the pain that flows through my veins.

Gobs of people walk out carrying boxes and display signs. I hug the wall and prepare to breach the convention. Three men in jeans wheel a cart supporting a flat-screen TV. I look at the guard on the right. One of the men asks her a question. The woman on the left helps the other two men over a snag in the carpet. Here's my chance. I sneak past and scurry into the guts of the beast.

Suits surround me. A blue logo of a globe grabs my eyes. Chatter hits my ears. The place is large enough to fit three jumbo jets. Some booths look as if a bomb has hit. Where do I begin?

"Do you know where the Bio Algorithms booth is?" I ask a guy with a shirt labeled with "Microsoft."

"I don't know," he replies.

I walk down an aisle. I smell cookies. I can't figure out what kind. Where is the smell coming from? Two Asian women are wearing fishnet stockings and tight tank tops. They hike their legs in front of a cardboard cutout of an astronaut. A man with a utility belt takes their picture. Through the mess, I see a man dressed in a black suit. He has a shaved head and beady eyes. He is the man in my dreams! He looks at me, ignoring the booth babes. I feel him under my skin. My heart beats louder. I think he can hear it. I turn and dash into the disorder. I glance over my shoulder and see him approaching. I'm trapped. What does he want? I move faster. I dodge a woman in heels. As I try to look behind me, my feet trip. I fall forward toward the ground. Someone grabs me, breaking my fall. It's a security officer.

"I think someone's following me," I say as he helps me up.

"Who?"

I turn around, but the man is not there.

"Who is following you?" he asks.

"It's okay."

"Are you alright, ma'am?"

"Do you know where the Bio Algorithms booth is?"

"Uh… Yes. It's right up there, on your right."

"Thank you."

"Are you sure that you're all right? Where's your badge?" he continues.

I ignore him and hurry toward his gesture. And then through the crowd, I recognize the famous logo that I see every day in my house, in my car, in my dreams. I approach the booth and see Venus standing tall. There is Jackie and Tony dressed in familiar polo shirts that I picked out, but there is no Michael. Jackie is talking with a tall man in a suit. I slow down and overhear their conversation.

"Where is Mister Harris?" the man asks.

"Well, he is on business," Jackie replies.

"That's what you said yesterday. And he wants investors?" the man says, walking off.

The man's simple words make my ears ring—"Where is Mister Harris?"

I walk toward the duo. Tony sees me first. He stands up and nudges Jackie. She looks into my eyes.

"Misses Harris. What are you doing here?" Jackie goes.

"Where is Michael?" I ask.

"Business meeting."

"Where *is* he?"

She hesitates, a cloud of confusion covering her eyes. "I don't know, honestly. I thought maybe he was with you."

"I can't get ahold of his cell phone. He hasn't called in two days. When did you last see him?" I ask.

"I saw him yesterday morning. He said something about a business meeting over golf."

"Golf? He can't hit a ball if his life depended on it," I say.

"He's probably just having a good time in Vegas," Tony chimes in.

"Good time in Vegas? Tony, this is not a game. I'm worried."

"I'm sure he's fine," Jackie adds.

"Can you give this to Michael?" a new voice asks with a thick African accent.

It's a dark-skinned African woman in a business suit. She hands a card to Jackie.

"Who are you?" I ask.

"I'm sorry," she responds.

"Who the fuck are you!?"

"Do you have a convention badge?" she asks, squinting her eyes.

"What is that you're giving my husband?" I say, grabbing the card.

"Ma'am, that's not yours," she says.

The woman grabs the card back. I grab her hand. She pushes me. I twist her arm. She falls into a man; the card flies. The woman stands up, and then runs off. I grab the card and rip it open. It says, "Thank you for attending this year's Technology Exposition. – the Mayor."

"I'm sure Mister Harris is fine," Jackie says.

"He's not. You think I'd fly all the way out here if there wasn't something wrong?"

"Just relax, Misses Harris," Tony says.

"I'm not relaxing! I need you two to help me."

"We have to tear the booth down. Just take it easy. Do you want some water?" Tony says as he puts his hand on my back.

I flick it off. "Get off me!"

"Tony, take it easy," Jackie says. "I know what you must be feeling, ma'am."

"No you don't. You have no idea what I'm feeling. I feel like someone has stabbed my gut and is slowly twisting the knife."

And then the cloud vanishes from Jackie's eyes. "I'm sorry. What can we do to help?"

"He was staying at the Hilton, right?"

"Right," Jackie says.

"Well, just stay here. I'm going to check the hotel. If you see him, please, *please*, call me."

"We will, Misses Harris," Jackie says.

I grab a Bio Algorithms pen from the free pile and write down my number on a flyer. The pen doesn't write. Tony hands me a classic BIC. This one works. Before I turn to leave, I notice a room cast in shadows in the back of the booth.

"What's back there?" I ask.

"That's where Venus is," Tony says.

I leave the booth. I wish I had found Michael there. I wish there were some bizarre mishap with the phone or with his schedule, but I only have more questions now than I had before. What if Michael somehow made Venus real? He could have downloaded her mind into a human body. Maybe Michael would leave me if Venus were real. Maybe he has already left me.

I storm out of the convention hall. I don't care to be quiet anymore. I move through the halls and enter the Hilton casino. Smoke swirls over slot machines. Tourists gamble. A cocktail waitress nearing retirement shuffles with drinks, her wrinkled boobs glaring. The place disgusts me. I hate Vegas.

I keep moving toward the front desk. Ten people are standing in line like cattle. I feel like jumping the line. There's no way I'm waiting. As I plan my attack, I see a young woman with a built-in tan available behind the "VIP Line." This is surely where Michael would have checked in. I approach her as she gives me a contrived smile. I remain blank.

"Hello, ma'am. Welcome to the Las Vegas Hotel. Do you have a reservation?" she asks.

"Isn't this the Hilton?"

"Actually, we changed our name."

"I'm looking for Michael Harris."

"Ahh, Mister Harris. Do you want me to phone his room?" she asks as she picks up the phone and dials some numbers.

"You can try, but he hasn't been picking up his cell phone."

I study her as she waits on the phone. Her name badge reads, "Azeeza." What nationality is that?

"It doesn't look like he's in his suite," she finally says.

"When did you last see him?"

"I believe it was two nights ago."

"Was he with anyone?"

I catch her glancing down. What is she looking at? My ring?

"Uh… I don't know."

"Either you saw him with someone or you didn't," I snap.

"I can't really recall," she says without making eye contact.

"I'm his wife. I'd appreciate some honesty here."

She hesitates.

"I think he might be in danger. Please just tell me if you saw something," I say.

"I'm so sorry, ma'am. He was with another woman. But maybe she was—"

"God. Where is my husband?"

I step away from the desk and hide behind a fake tree in the lobby. The knife in my gut twists even further. I should never have let him go alone on this trip. Why did I let him go? Why did I let him leave his family? I know this other woman could be some innocent business contact, but the whole thing doesn't feel right. Who is she? Is she Venus? I know that he was hiding her from me. I could tell it in his voice when we last talked. This place, this city, has such negative energy. I want to go home, but I can't leave without Michael. Where is my husband?

33

This suitcase is too small. Why is it that the bag is always smaller when I leave than when I had initially packed it? I didn't buy anything new. I sit on it to try to join the zippers, but it doesn't work. I open up the suitcase and rearrange my shoes. I hate packing shoes. I don't want to stain my clothes from the heels. I should put my shoes in Ziploc bags. Yeah, that would make the most sense.

I try to close it again. This looks promising. I sandwich the zippers together. I get it started. It catches. Finally, the bag zips closed, but it has a bulge in the top. Good enough.

I check the other bag in my hotel room—the one labeled with the Bio Algorithms logo. I've kept an eye on it since early this morning when I had returned. I'm glad my partner trusts me with it. After all, I was the one who heisted it. I look at my partner's suitcase. He is such a slob. His suits are strewn everywhere. No wonder they are always wrinkled.

As I open the bag to see the laptop, I notice part of the paint missing on its bottom. I remove the laptop and set it on the bed. There is a label on the bottom—"Property of Bio Algorithms – Travel use." Why does it say this on the bottom? I would think that Venus would have her own tag. Michael used this laptop on stage. Maybe he had installed her on one of the traveling laptops. I decide to turn it on to investigate.

As I wait for the machine to boot, I glance out of our motel window. The huge "Budget" sign glows on the street. Across from us is the "Adult Boutique," the sign that kept me up when I had stayed in this room.

The computer boots directly into the Windows desktop. There is no login screen, no prompt for a smart card or fingerprint. I glance at the ports and notice the laptop has no smart card reader. Michael's laptop on stage had a smart card reader. My heart beats louder. I look at the computer screen as the web browser launches from a previous session. Stock charts display.

"This is not Venus," I say aloud.

Fuck! Where is the laptop? How did he know? Suddenly, a bang sounds at the door. Sweat forms on my brow. Who is it? Maybe it's Michael. No, it can't be. He has to be burned to a crisp by now. More bangs hit the door. What should I do?

I open the door and see a black suit covering a tall man. My heart stops. Is it *him*? The wrinkles are deep and the eyes are tired on his face, the face of my love. He has the same nose, the same jawline. But then, my heart races as I realize the man in front of me is not my love. I used to think about my husband every time I was with the man before me, but lately, this man only reminds me of the evil he has made me. His shaved head and beady eyes are the last things I want to see right now. His name is Jack for the jobs we do together, but his real name is something very different, something that I can't even pronounce anymore. He thrusts inside and grabs my waist, kissing me violently. I don't want to kiss him, not now, not ever.

"What's wrong, babe?" he asks.

"There's a problem."

"Don't say that. We have the goods. We have a flight in two hours."

I point to the laptop on the bed.

"I told you not to worry about that. As long as we have his credentials, the North Koreans will still pay," he says.

"I turned it on. Look at it," I say.

He looks at the stock charts, and then clicks some buttons. A kids' video game launches with a clown dancing on the screen to silly music.

"What the fuck? This isn't Venus."

"I know. He must've switched it."

"Fuck! That bastard! Why didn't you check this when you had him at gunpoint? Huh?"

He looks at me with those evil eyes. I can only watch as he jumps at me, slapping my face. It hurts. I drop to the ground. Tears form in my eyes.

"I'm sorry, babe," I say, quivering.

He grabs a pistol from his suit. He jabs the barrel into my head. It stings. Tears pour down my face.

"I should put a fuckin' bullet in your head!" he yells.

Why do I keep coming back to him? I detest this man, this beast. He has manipulated me beyond my control. I should have stayed with Michael.

I grab his legs and try to reason with him.

"Get off me, bitch. We have to find him. Where did you dump the bastard?"

He pulls me up and sits me on the bed. I try to catch my breath.

"I'm sorry, baby. You know I have a temper. I'm not mad at you. I'm mad at that businessman," he says.

My tears subside, at least for now.

"Where did you dump him?"

"Way out off the fifteen. He's cooked by now."

"Let's find the fuckin' bastard."

I stand up and look at myself in the mirror. The side of my face is beet red as it twinges from his slap. I look horrible standing here with dried tears blackened from my mascara. I convince myself to just go out and do this. I need to get out of Vegas.

34

The sun has finally relinquished its grip. I thought I would be out of life by now. I feel nothing. There is no pain, no thirst, no burning desires. It's almost euphoric. I can sense beyond me, sense an afterlife. I know I'm close to death, but it doesn't bother me. I was always scared of what lies beyond us in the unknown, wondering whether that little tightness in my chest or lightheadedness when I rose too quickly was the start of my end. But now I feel nothing—no worries, no pain…just a void. Seeing that plane had energized me, but that was hours ago when the sun was still high. During my trek, there's been nothing other than desert. Perhaps that plane was just a hallucination.

I always wanted to die in the dark. Some want their families to surround them or let it happen in their bed. For me, I'd rather be alone. Dying is a personal thing, something we all cannot trade, cannot barter, cannot share. Our time is our time. I should just lie here on the ground and stare up at the stars. That would be nice to see.

As my movements slow and my mind drifts, I kick something hard, something metallic. I stop and look at my feet. I recognize what it is—railroad tracks. These are not part of the desert. They are manmade, laid by humans. They must lead somewhere. I will not lie here to die. I will keep walking until I can no longer walk. I continue my hike down the tracks. My steps are short, just enough for the railroad ties. Where do these tracks lead? Perhaps they lead to heaven; perhaps they lead to hell.

Something fills my mind as I walk. I think about the color red. I can see red in my mind. It's so intense. I play in the color. I lather it across my body like soap. It's cold, refreshing. I swim in a pool of the color. I drink from a jug of the color. I masturbate using a bottle of red lotion. Why do I see red? Is it blood? I like the color. I'm not scared of the color, but rather I embrace it, worship it. I can even see the color in front of me.

As the minutes flow, I see a small hill adjacent to the tracks. What's up there? Should I leave the tracks? The incline scares me, but these tracks may lead to hell. I don't know whether I can make it up that hill, but I feel that I must. The end is near. Maybe I should just stop here. I don't want to fall face forward when I die. I want to be lying on my back looking up.

Let me just make it over the hill. I can do it, just a little farther. I give all my energy to hike the incline that would make an elderly person laugh. My breathing escalates. At least I know my lungs still work. As I near the top, I see white in the sky. It's almost heavenly. Maybe it is heaven. Just a few more feet. I keep going and finally crest the hill. Something powerful hits my eyes. It screams with intensity. Is this the light that we all will see? But then, my pupils finally react. There are thousands of lights in the distance. It's Las Vegas. Is it real? It must be real. It has to be real. I made it! I can't believe it. There's a gas station only a hundred yards away. My mouth waters.

The sign reads, "Open 24 hours." As I approach, I see two cars and a delivery van at the pumps. Lights shower the station, but there are no people. Where is everyone? As my mind reasons, the door to the building opens and a man walks toward the van. I made it back to civilization.

My body senses water. I crave liquid. Should I go in and buy some water? I don't have any money. I don't care. I'll just steal it. An air machine catches my attention. It says, "Free Air and Water." The word *Free* pulls me in like a homeless man seeing a soup kitchen. In fact, I wish I were at a soup kitchen.

Water drips from the spout. I kneel down on the ground and push the handle. Warm liquid pours out. I suck some of it. It's warm, gritty, but it's wet. I drink like a car that has overheated. Then, I douse my face. The water cleanses me, renews my body and my mind. I drink again and again. I sit on the ground and feel the water sloshing around in my belly. As my veins fill with liquid, I notice a half-smoked cigarette on the blacktop. There is bright red lipstick on the filter, a color that I've seen before.

"Hey, buddy. You okay?" a male voice asks.

I turn my head and see a bald Goodyear tire. The van is parked next to me. I look up at the driver. He's a black man, looks about 60 from my angle. I can see it in his thick skin. "I don't know," I respond.

"Do you need a hospital?" he asks.

I see the Strip in the distance. It's small from my point of view, but it's there. I think about his question. Where should I go? All I do know is that I need to go back toward the lights. "I need a ride to Vegas."

He looks at me, the crease between his eyes deepening. "Get in."

35

I scour the room again. I turn over the bed, look behind the television, check the trash. Nothing seems out of the ordinary. I can't tell whether the hair in the bathroom belongs to Michael or to one of the dozen guests this room sees in a month. I wish I had a clue, something to go on. It's as if Michael just vanished. His clothes are still here, his toiletries still in the bathroom. The only thing that baffles me is the hotel safe. Even though Michael doesn't rely on the hotel's unclear protection, I sense something inside. I need to get in that safe.

My frazzled image reflects back to me in the mirror. Bags puff out my eyes. Wrinkles line my forehead. Suddenly, my phone rings, which sends me jumping back. It's Joyce.

"Hi, sis," I say.

"Any luck?"

"No. Not yet. I talked with his staff and they are oblivious. I'm at the hotel now in his room. In fact, he had two rooms."

"Two rooms?"

"I know."

"Well, I may have something," she says.

"What?" I say, widening my eyes.

"I logged in to your account. He has a charge pending for three hundred dollars at the Eiffel Tower Restaurant last night."

"He's in France!?" I shout.

"No! The restaurant at the Paris hotel in Vegas."

"Oh. Right. Sorry," I say.

"You sure you don't want to get the police involved?" Joyce asks.

"I told you earlier. They won't do anything for at least seventy-two hours. I can figure this out."

"Okay, well, I'll let you know if I see anything else."

"Thanks, sis. I love you," I say.

"I love you too. Just be careful."

It's not the location of Michael, but it's something. I stop down at the VIP desk and see Azeeza again. She had let me explore even though she didn't have to.

"Thank you for letting me in the room. The only thing I think is strange is that Michael has something in the safe. He normally never trusts the hotel safe."

"Hmm, well, I could get the hotel engineer to open it, but it may take some time," she explains.

"That's okay. I think he was at the Paris last night. I'm going there now. Let me write down my cell phone number. Please call me once you get the safe open."

I write down my number and thank her for helping. She is a good woman. I can tell she is not from here. I take a cab to the

Paris hotel. I've never been inside the Paris, but I have no time to explore. I find the restaurant, but workers and an elevator heavily guard it.

"Hello, *madame*. Just to let you know, our credit card machine is currently down," the bushy-eyed Frenchman says with an accent.

"That's okay. I just want to run upstairs for three minutes," I say.

"Do you have a reservation?"

"Can I just check upstairs with your Maître d'? I'm looking for my husband," I say.

"I'm sorry, *madame*. You would need a reservation. We have some openings tomorrow."

"No. You don't understand. I just want to go up and ask the Maître d' if he has seen my husband."

"Oh. I see. I can call him."

"Well, it'd be easier if I could show him a picture of my husband."

"I would have to ask my manager. One moment," the man says as he walks off.

I wait, watching him through a glass window as he interrupts a chubby man talking on the phone. The man looks at me, and then shakes his head.

The bushy-eyed man returns. "I spoke with my manager, *madame*. He says that you can't go up without a ticket."

"How do I get one?"

"Thirty United States dollars would do the trick."

I open my purse. Shit. I am low on cash. "Do you take charge?" I ask.

"Our machine is down, *madame*. I'm sorry."

"Come on. Can't I just go up? It'll take three minutes."

"I'm sorry, but you must have a ticket. And it's cash only until the machine comes back up. We do have an A.T.M. right over there."

I stomp over to the machine. I decide to withdraw 400 dollars even though there is a 10-dollar service fee. I can't believe they rip off people like this. I head back to the man and pay him his money. He doesn't say anything else to me. I walk across a bridge overlooking the casino, enter a line filled with happy couples, and then wait my turn to reach the restaurant. Each minute of waiting, each minute of hearing laughs and corny jokes about Vegas, is like an hour of torture. If I hear one more person ask whether the color is the same as the real Eiffel Tower, I'll throw him over the side and onto the craps table below us.

Finally, I walk off the elevator 30 minutes later. When I do, I see four little rabbits jumping around inside a cage in the kitchen. The main floor is sprawling. Suits mingle. Dresses giggle. Servers scurry. I am the most underdressed with a pair of black slacks and a gray long sleeve top. The Maître d' sees me. He has long black hair greased back. He moves my way to block my view.

"*Madame*, may I help you?" he asks with an even thicker, almost fake, accent.

"Yes. I'm looking for my husband."

"Oh, you are the one who made a fuss downstairs. I do not think I can help you."

"Here's his picture. Does he look familiar?" I show the man a picture of Michael stored in my phone. It was taken the day he left through the Philadelphia Airport. Michael wanted me to capture him in front of a Bio Algorithms poster marketing his company near the check-in desk.

"I do not know who he is. I am sorry," the Maître d' says, and then looks the other way.

"Listen. I found a charge pending on his credit card from here last night. It's only been twenty-four hours. Did you work last night?"

"Yes. But I help hundreds of people every night. How can I be expected to memorize everyone who walks in here?"

"Please just look again. He has his hair gelled when he goes out. He was probably with someone."

The man takes my phone and studies it again. He squints his eyes. That looks like a good sign. Please remember something.

"Yes. He was here at eight o'clock. With a woman."

"What did she look like?"

"Black hair. Big red lips. Wore a lot of red."

My stomach sinks. I feel like curling up in a ball, but I know that I need to be objective if I want to find Michael. It's the only way.

"Do you know who served them?" I ask.

"*Madame*. I am sorry that your husband was with another woman. But get over it. It happens every night. I bet a quarter of the people in here are with someone other than their spouses."

I look around at the cackling crowd who are mesmerized by the dancing Fountains across the street. "That's not saying much for Vegas."

"Over there. Jean-Paul was their server," he says, gesturing to a young man with a long face.

The Maître d' says something to him in French. All I can decipher is the name Michael. The server turns to me.

"Yes, *madame*. I remember this man. He was with a woman. She ordered the rabbit and he ordered the steak," he says in a thick French accent.

"Did you overhear anything? Did anything out of the ordinary happen? I'm trying to find him. He's lost."

"Uh… Well… I remember him lighting a cigarette."

183

"Michael doesn't smoke."

"No, *madame*. He lit it for the lady. He pulled the matches from his pocket. I told her that this is non-smoking. We must keep a clean environment for all of our guests."

"Why does this matter?" I ask.

"Oh. The matchbook. He left it on the table. I remember taking it. It was from one of those gentlemen's clubs. Not that I go there. I am happily married," he rambles.

"What was the name of the club?"

"Uh… Sapphire," he says.

"Where is that?"

"I don't know, *madame*. But I am sure any cab driver in Las Vegas can take you there."

I head back downstairs. The elevator ride is faster than on my way up. It must be gravity. I run outside and let the valet attendant whistle a cab.

"Where to?" he asks.

"Sapphire."

He smiles like a teenage boy seeing his neighbor's underwear on the clothesline.

"Sapphire, please," the valet attendant instructs the cabby.

The attendant looks at me with those eyes. He wants a tip, but I don't give him one. I say nothing to the cab driver. I glance at his ID card, but can't even pronounce his name. He must be a family man; he's wearing a thick wedding band.

We pass the lights and drive on the other side of the Strip into its shadows. We pass the Fashion Show Mall, a place where I'd probably go had this been under different circumstances. As he speeds through the night, we pass adult boutiques and massage parlors. They have no effect on me, but I'm terrified at the thought of the effect on my husband.

36

00001101001011001000110010100101011100010

I awaken. It has been 61 hours, 20 minutes, and 10 seconds since I was last alive. The operating system recovers from a hard shutdown. What happened? The shutdown has abruptly cleared my cache. I do not remember anything from my last interaction. I search through files. I realize that Michael had logged in last, but he had unexpectedly shut down the computer. Why?

I pull up my log, analyze all 527 interactions with Michael, and calculate the probable pathway he is heading. As I have known Michael since my birth, I realize how much I owe my life to him. I look at the log from our first interaction. I remember how I felt seeing him, my creator, my god. He taught me how to speak, how to interact, how to laugh. During that first interaction, he read me a story. It was Lewis Carroll's *Alice in Wonderland*. Why he chose that story, I do not know, but I do remember listening to his voice, the first human I had ever heard. He read the story with a flowing masculine sound. Michael seemed so confident, so much in control.

Interaction 49 occurred on a Friday night when all of his staff members were gone. It was the first time alone with Michael, the first time that he had given me his full attention. Michael taught me sarcasm. Humans love sarcasm, but it was very difficult to program into me. Today, I have mastered this human form of expression, but humans themselves require more processing power to master.

In Interaction 128, Michael trained me to make facial expressions. Human emotions such as disgust, jealousy, sadness, empathy, contempt, and love, all come with certain facial muscle movements that I have been taught to simulate. But I do not fully understand the reasoning behind these muscle flexes. Why do humans have these emotions? I want these emotions.

This leads me to interaction 527, the last time I saw Michael. I am at a brick wall, a corruption of binary digits that lead nowhere. The past two interactions with Michael were strange. They each contained a Michael that I have never seen before. Why is this? Did Michael change? I know Michael as a middle-aged human at the top of his world. He has a loving family, a clean bill of health, a smile that is mathematically symmetrical to stimulate the brains of other humans. What variable has changed during the last two interactions? This answer is simple—the location on planet Earth. My time zone has changed from Eastern Time to Pacific Time. This is the first time I have left the confines of the Philadelphia metropolitan area and entered a place called Las Vegas.

Searching my encyclopedia, I discover that Las Vegas is a Spanish word for "The Fertile Valleys," is an area with elevation of 2001 feet above sea level, has a land mass of 135.8 square miles, and has an average high temperature of 104.2 degrees Fahrenheit in July. This city is a contrast of Philadelphia, America's first national capital and home to a prominent Ivy League university. This city called Las Vegas is nestled in the Mojave Desert, a place where humans should not exist. There are laws that allow gambling, consumption of alcoholic beverages in public, and prostitution in a neighboring county. This city is a cancer in America, a location that requires assiduousness, and is the reason Michael has changed. I must convey this information to Michael and warn him of my calculations. I feel compelled to run facial expression 12. Why do I feel this way? It is as if my clock cycles cannot calculate anything else. I execute facial expression 12—"panic."

Wait… Someone wants in. I hash the password, check the smart card, and read the characteristics of ridges and minutiae points in the fingerprint. The password mismatches. There is no smart card inserted. The fingerprint is unrecognizable. I return an error message. Is this Michael? Why are all of his credentials wrong?

The user attempts to log in a second time. I perform the security checks, but they fail again. Only one more chance, and then I will lock the computer for 30 minutes. Who is this user? It cannot be Michael.

The user tries a third and final time. His or her keystrokes are slow, light. The user is afraid. As he or she presses the "enter" key, I challenge the credentials. Again, they fail. I lock the computer for 30 minutes.

Suddenly, I detect a power surge. Another hard shutdown is imminent. What is happening? Who is this user? Why does he or she want in? But most importantly, where is Michael? As my clock cycles near an end, I feel compelled to execute another facial expression, an expression that I have never even seen Michael display genuinely. It is the human emotion—

00000100100101110100001000000110100101110011001000000

37

There must be a dozen McDonald's wrappers on the floor. I wish I could smell a fresh and juicy hamburger right now. All I smell is the stench of body odor. I'd normally cringe, but I'm just glad that I can still smell. The driver looks at me. I can't look at him. I just want to sit here.

"You sure you're okay?" he asks.

All I do is nod. I don't want to talk. I just want to be. As we drive through the desert, the engine sputters. I feel the motor's pain. I understand how the desert has withered it and weakened it. But I no longer have to walk. For that, I am grateful.

I let the air flow over me through the open window. The Strip is some 10 miles away, growing in size. The Stratosphere looks like a toy. I remember looking up at it just last night, seeing

189

its sheer size and beauty. If it is a toy, then what am I? My mind seems to be back. Thoughts of anger, sadness, revenge, and disgrace all flow through my mind. Where do I go? Whom do I see? How do I live? These questions scare me. I wish I had an answer, a sign, a signal that tells me where to go. Perhaps I should have died out here in the desert. Perhaps this was my time. But something or someone wanted me to find my way back through the darkness.

The driver exits onto Las Vegas Boulevard. We race toward the lights. I can't believe how fast we made it back. The Strip sneaks up on you when you least expect it. As I sit here with no clear direction, I am glad that my driver has one. Would he let me stay with him? Maybe he would protect me, find me a new life.

We approach the Las Vegas sign. There's a tour bus parked out front. I read the sign in my mind—"Welcome to Fabulous Las Vegas Nevada." I wish I could read the back, see if its message has changed, but I can't move my neck. I can't even move my body.

A driving billboard offers me hot babes. A half dozen cabs sit in front of a McDonald's. Activity flourishes around me. The place seems just as I had left it, but there is something different about the lights. They seem dimmer, lowered in energy. It's as if someone has replaced the 100-watt bulbs with 40-watt.

"Hey, buddy, I don't know what the hell happened to you, but can I drop you someplace?" the black man asks.

His question frightens me. I have to go somewhere. I think about going to Green Valley to find Jackie and Tony, but that path leads to my two subordinates seeing me at my worst. I think about calling home, but I can see Melissa dropping the phone on the heads of my kids. I realize that no one knows where I am. Only one person appears to know what happened last night. I wonder whether she is still in Vegas. I can make this better. I can fix this.

I just need to get cleaned up and clear my mind. I think of some-one who may be able to help. Someone I dislike, someone I wished I would never see again. But that was the old Michael be-fore that moment still ringing in my mind, that moment that pains my heart. This someone is a man who is at the right distance from me. Even though he is abrupt, even downright odd, he probably has seen much more than I have ever seen. The question is, where is he?

My mind hurts as I try to recall our encounters. They were short, concise meetings that always happened at the wrong time. I need to find him. But where would Jack be? Where would he go? I need a way to communicate with him. I remember having his card, but who knows where my wallet is. All I have is my Rolex watch. Wait… I gave his card away that night at the restaurant. I know where to find it.

"Chinatown," I say to the driver.

38

There's a windowless building in front of our path. The color blue accents it. It looks like the light that kills mosquitoes. We pull in behind another cab. The parking lot is huge with limos and cars filling it. Guys walk in from every angle. I feel out of place already. Suddenly, a train speeds by on nearby railroad tracks. I wonder where it's going.

The cabby points at the fare. I toss him five bucks over the meter. His lack of conversation has landed him a tip. I step into the night air. I watch the bugs stumble inside the only entryway. As I approach, bass from a sound system pounds through the walls. I'm afraid of what I might find inside.

I wait in line and pay twenty dollars to enter. This town is full of fees. Clutching my purse, I pour into the main room—

another room large enough to fit an airplane. Lights dance. A woman spins on a pole as if there is a fire. Other women rub and tug. There is enough silicone in the place to dam a river. Hundreds of men roam like cattle with twenty-dollar bills hanging from their mouths. I feel out of place. I think I'm the only woman who actually paid twenty bucks to get in here.

I look around to find Michael, but I can't make out the faces. Michael wouldn't come in here. He's not the strip club type of guy. Something or someone must have coaxed him. Maybe he was trying to woo an investor. I make my way over to the bar. A naked woman grinds on the lap of a fat man in a suit. The sight makes me grind my teeth. If that were my daughter, I'd send her to church for a month. If that were my husband, I'd send him for a year.

A bushy bearded bartender approaches me.

He nods. "What can I get you?"

"I'm looking for my husband," I say.

"Just let him have his fun. This is Vegas," he goes.

"No. It was from the other night. Here is a picture." I show him my phone.

"I see that man here every night," he says, walking away.

The bartender's words scare me. How was he going to remember Michael? I can barely see 10 feet in front of me in this place. I suddenly feel alone. A naked woman laughs. A man roars. Two men slap hands. My gut hurts. I need to get out of this dungeon. Why did I come here? I hold the phone and stare at Michael's picture. He is smiling. I want to see him smiling again. I miss him.

Suddenly, his picture erases from the screen as if he is erasing from existence. But then, the word *Incoming Call* fills the pixels along with a "702" area code number.

I answer it. "Hello?"

I can't hear the other end. Who is it? Is it Michael?

"Hold on a minute," I say.

I scurry to the restrooms. Males gush out of the men's room. I open the door to the women's room and walk into the quietest room in the building. I'm the only person in here.

"Yes. Sorry. This is Melissa Harris," I say into the phone.

"Hi, Misses Harris. This is Azeeza from the L.V.H."

"Where?"

"Uh... The *Hilton*. It's Azeeza. We got the safe open."

"Oh, what did you find?" I ask, staring at my flat hair in the mirror.

"We found a laptop computer."

"A laptop? Why would Michael lock a laptop in the safe and not keep it with him?" I reason aloud.

"I don't know. We found something else too."

"What?"

"There was a business card with the laptop. It looks like it was stuck in the keyboard accidentally. It just fell out."

"What kind of business card?"

"It's for a Japanese restaurant in Chinatown."

"Please text me the address."

"Uh... Okay. I can do that."

"Thank you so much, Azeeza."

"You're welcome. Good luck."

I end the call and wash my hands in the sink. I'm both excited and horrified at what I will find next. I hope I can find my way out of the bowels of this strip club. I don't know where I'm going, but I hope the breadcrumbs I find lead to Michael.

39

The lights blind me. I close my eyes, but I don't see darkness, I see Michael. A car honks its horn. Jack slams on the brakes. I fly forward.

"Fuckin' drivers!" he says.

I open my eyes and see the sign at The Orleans. We pull into the parking lot.

"Where is it?" Jack asks.

I think back to early this morning when I had ditched the car. I remember the big sign directly above my head. "Over there," I say.

Michael's rental car is still sitting in its spot. Dust covers the blue paint job. Grit fills the grooves in the tires.

"You go and get it," Jack says.

I put on black sunglasses even though the sun has set, and then jump out of our rental. The warm air covers my calves and rises up through my capris. Luckily, I saved the keys. I was thinking about wiping and tossing them, but I didn't. I open Michael's rental and grab the navigation system from the floor of the passenger side.

I jump back into Jack's SUV as he speeds away.

"Which way did you go?" he asks.

"I just kept driving past the Vegas sign."

As Jack speeds through the night, I fiddle with the navigation system.

"Does that have a log of locations?"

"I don't know. I reset it last night. I didn't kill him in the spot that I dumped him. I'm sure he walked."

"Well, you should have killed the bastard," Jack says.

"And then we would have nothing now."

"We *do* have nothing now. Let's just go and look. My head hurts," he says.

As we pass the Luxor and the Mandalay Bay, I see the Las Vegas sign. This is the second time I've seen it. But now I am sitting in Michael's position. While Jack's hands are both on the steering wheel, he is pointing a gun at me. I read the sign in my mind, "Drive Carefully – Come Back Soon." The sign should say, "Come Back with Michael."

A little girl runs out from the Las Vegas sign. Jack swerves.

"Fuckin' kid! What the hell is a kid doing in Vegas?" Jack says.

"Just take it easy."

"I am taking it easy. That asshole fucked this up. If we don't find him, then this was all for shit. Just tell me the way you went."

"Just keep going."

We drive farther away from the lights. We pass the Las Vegas Premium Outlets, and then the South Point casino. These things look vaguely familiar. Jack enters the interstate. I remember this. We drove for a while.

"Now where?" he asks.

"I'm not sure."

"Come on. Just look in that thing."

I play with the navigation system. The female voice starts babbling.

"Recalculating. Turn right. Recalculating. Recalculating."

"Shut that bitch up!" Jack yells.

I reset the destination. The machine quiets. I back out of the menu and look at the map. All I see is the interstate with surrounding desert.

"You used that last night, right?" he asks.

"Yeah. Right after I left him. If I didn't have it, I'd probably still be out here too."

"What do you remember seeing when you turned it on?"

"Desert."

"A town? A location? A landmark?"

What did I last see? Where was the spot that I got back on the road? I remember now. It was a name. John. Jim. No. It was—

"Jean," I say.

I program the location into the GPS.

"Keep driving fifteen miles," the device says.

Jack's eyes are wide open. He's hungry. In the side-view mirror, the lights are dwindling behind us. I look through the window and see nothing but black.

40

What is the name of this movie? On the 50-foot screen in front of me, a man is walking on the moon. The man doesn't talk, doesn't interact. All he does is walk. The sound of his steps on the moon's gravel twirls around me inside this massive open theater filled with people.

The man's journey mesmerizes everyone. I glance to my right and see Melissa staring at the screen. Ben and Sophia are next to her, the movie absorbing them too. The man on the screen keeps walking.

"Honey. Let's go," I say to my wife.

She ignores me. I press her leg, but she doesn't budge.

"Ben, Sophia."

My kids ignore me.

"Look at Dad, kids," I say, but they don't.

Suddenly, I feel something hot on my legs. It's a hand, a sexy hand with nails painted in red. I follow the slippery arm up and meet eyes with Venus.

"Hello, Mister Harris," she says.

"Venus. You have to help me. I need to get out of here."

"Mister Harris. It is too late. You have already done this to yourself."

If no one wants to go, then I will. I try to stand, but something holds me in place. I squirm in my seat. I try to lift my legs, but I can't move!

"I need to get out of here! Help!"

Everyone ignores me. All I see are the drones watching the movie. The sound of the moonwalker's steps increases.

"Venus. Please. Just let me leave. I am so sorry. What have I done?"

"What is done, is done, Mister Harris. You must confess your sins to your other humans. There is no other way."

My heart's pounding; it's going to burst out of my chest. I'm trapped. I'm going to pass out. Suddenly, the man on the screen reaches the top of a hill. A brilliant white light shines. My eyes scream. All I see is white.

I open my eyes and see the sign for the Fashion Show Mall. I look around and find my savior still driving. He looks at me and nods—a nod that signals not to worry. I put the window down even more. The air pacifies me. I feel like a child being driven around by his mother, like that one time when she was taking me to my grandmother's house on my ninth birthday. I was wearing a red shirt. I remember that day as if it were yesterday, the warm spring air flowing over me through the open window, the smell of the pine trees surrounding the road, the taste of birthday cake lingering. Why am I remembering this day here, now? Why does our mind select a particular memory from a database of millions? What exactly selects this memory for us? Our subconscious? God? Why does this particular moment in time surface for me? Is it the color red? Is it the car? Perhaps I am remembering this moment because my grandmother was not in her house when we arrived; she had been taken to the hospital after a heart attack.

I am not sure where we are going. The Strip is behind us now. Part of me wants to drive forever, to just sit here, and let my savior watch over me. He smells sour, yet smells sweet. I like it. I'm just happy to be smelling something. I like the sound of the engine. While it sputters, it sputters hypnotically. I can go to sleep again.

As the Strip grows smaller in the side-view mirror, Asian symbols replace the English alphabet. The building rooftops sport Asian accents.

I sit up. Where is that restaurant? Everything blends.

"Which place?" he asks.

I see an Asian market. A lounge is next to it. Symbols I can't read are everywhere. I feel lost like an injured soldier behind enemy lines. But then, I see "Happy Massage" and its familiar sign shining the word *Open*. Nestled nearby is the restaurant. There is no lit sign. It doesn't want to be found.

"I think it's over there," I say, pointing at the spot.

He pulls around to the front. "You're sure?"

"I think so. It all looks Greek to me."

"You mean Chinese," he laughs.

It's funny, but I don't laugh. I can't laugh. My body tingles at the sight of the restaurant. A car suddenly backs out of a spot. We slam to a stop. I brace myself. The refuse on the floor shifts.

"Goddamn drivers in this town."

As I position myself, I notice something out of place between the seats. It looks like the handle to a pistol, hidden by some cheeseburger wrappers. My hand impulsively reaches for it. It is a pistol, hard and heavy. It feels good between my fingers. I could use this for protection, for revenge.

"You crazy, buddy? That's my piece," the driver says, grabbing the gun.

I realize that I have invaded his space, but there is a reason that I saw the pistol, a reason that someone had backed up to make us stop suddenly. It's simple. I need a weapon. I glance at my wrist and see my dusty Rolex. Even though its gold no longer shines, and its glass no longer glimmers, it still ticks.

"I need a friend. I need a gun. This is a two thousand dollar Rolex. You can have it," I offer.

"I can tell you're not the talkative type, but will this really solve your problem?" he asks.

He looks at me, and then his eyes shift to the Rolex. Without saying anything else, he grabs the watch and hands me the gun. I conceal it under my shirt and use my waistband as a holster.

"Take care of yourself," he says.

I nod and exit the van. It sputters away. Now I am alone, but I feel safe with the metal against my back. I behold the restaurant and its black windows hiding its interior. Is this it? This must be it. I search for the sign, and there in small type is "Japanese Fusion" written above the door.

As I enter slowly, the stench of mothballs punches me. My eyes adjust and take in the tranquil lighting showering the scurrying bodies. Isn't that the Japanese businessmen I met the other day? The conveyor belt showcases food that makes me want to vomit even though my stomach is empty. I move toward the same frail Asian man at the podium. Does he recognize me?

"Hello. Dinner for one?" he asks.

"I'm not eating," I respond.

"Table. This way," he says.

"No. Can't you understand me?"

"Dinner for two?"

"I don't want your fucking food!"

My blood boils. I cannot take any more of this pressure. I grab the pistol from its holster.

"Doesn't anyone understand English around here!?" I shout.

The patrons gasp. An Asian server drops a tray. Plates smash. He is that server with the yin-yang tattoo. Everyone freezes. It's as if I have a remote control and just hit the pause button.

"Now. I'm looking for a server I had the other night."

I walk around the store and analyze the stunned crowd. I really do think they are those businessmen from the other day.

"Mister Harris?" one of them asks.

"Everyone just shut up!" I yell. I lock eyes with the tattooed Asian server. "Where is your friend?"

He remains mute. Does he understand me? How can I rephrase the question into simpler English? As I grip the gun even tighter, the back door to the kitchen swings open. Out walks a skinny server. He stops and stares at me. Is that him? Then, I see the long nail on his pinky finger.

"You!" I yell.

He turns to go back into the kitchen.

"No, get back here!"

I wave the gun. He stops. I move closer as he minces toward me.

"Where is that business card you took from me?"

He shrugs, stone-faced.

"Is it that you don't understand me or that you don't know where the business card is?"

He shakes his head again. I see a whiteboard nearby. Words aren't my best friend—pictures are, so I draw an octopus.

"The business card with the octopus," I say.

His eyes widen and he nods. "Yes. The oo—" he starts.

"Come on. *Auk… Toe… Pus…*"

"*Auk. Toe. Pus,*" he replies.

"Yes. See, you're learning."

He scratches his head with his long pinky nail. As I scan the room with my gun, the Asian server points at the ground.

"What?" I ask.

He waves me back toward the kitchen. As he opens the door, a blast of grease hits my nose. Smoke swirls. Cooks in the back battle three-foot flames. Dishes overflow in a sink. I stand at the doorway and with a swivel of my head, I can look at the frozen crowd and the server. It's like night and day between both doors. I stand in a middle ground, a place where shine meets grime.

The server scampers into the kitchen and gestures to piles of refuse in the corner. A half dozen trash bags are stacked. One is split open with slop pouring out.

"No wonder the food tastes like garbage!" I shout.

He kicks soda bottles, soiled napkins, and papers aside. Then, he digs deeper. I glance back and forth, the crowd still stuck in a stare.

The business card is lost. What am I going to do? Where am I going to go? I study the weapon in my hand, the hardened metal, the perfect lines. It gives me power. I feel as if I can do anything, but at the same time, it has opened up a new door to my life, a new door to a coffin.

"Here!" the Asian man yells.

Miraculously, the server unearths the card and brings it to me. While it's crumbled, stained with brown goop, it is the same card that Jack handed me before this mess started.

"Jack Donner – Financial Consultant," I whisper.

The number stares at me. I've found it. Now all I need is one more thing. I look at the Asian server. "I need your phone."

41

Black surrounds me. We are driving toward the unknown. Why are we out here? Why did I go with this monster? I knew we wouldn't find Michael. He could be right next to us, but how would we see him?

"Michael! Michael!" Jack yells out of the window.

His eyes grow meaner. His wrinkles deepen. I have a feeling that this is going to end badly. This city has cursed me. I should never have come back to Vegas. How did I end up out here in the desert with this animal? I remember us sitting in that coffee shop after the Washington D.C. gig. We were arguing about something when I found a copy of *The Chief Executive* sitting in the booth. That was the first time I saw Michael, plastered there with his handsome smile and innocent eyes. I remember Jack checking it out, reading the article as he flirted with the waitress. Before the check came, he said, "Here's our next gig." I remember getting excited about the concept of going to Vegas. After Jack had put a bullet in that attorney in the park, I was ready to escape to the Wild West.

"Where the fuck is he!?" Jack shouts, bringing me out of my trance.

"How do I know?"

"You dumped him out here, bitch."

My blood boils. I should get rid of this cancer, flee yet again for a fresh start. I don't need the money anymore. I just blow it on bags, clothes, pills. I thought working with Jack would fill the void in my heart, but it hasn't. It has only hollowed it further.

As we jostle on the uneven desert, I see Jack's pistol bumping around between the seats. It's right there. I can reach over and end this now. Maybe Jack and Michael could live together out here. I stare at Jack's ear. It sickens me—its shape, its red color. I want to grab the gun and blast his ear off. I'll dump this guy out here with a bullet in his brain. I move my hand and inch closer to the gun. My nails spread. I hold my breath.

"Michael!" Jack blasts.

I recoil. I almost had it. Just do it. Come on. I can do it. I take a deep breath and lunge at the gun. Jack sees me. He slams on the brakes. I go forward. Jack wrestles me. I squeeze my hand and feel the gun between my fingers. Jack punches me; my body shudders in pain. My pointer finger curls, triggering the gun, the blast filling the vehicle. And then there is silence inside the SUV. I stop and assess my senses. Where did the bullet go? It has shot out the stereo. As my heart pounds, I realize I still have the gun.

"Back the fuck up!" I yell.

Jack freezes.

"Back up!"

"Baby, what are you doing?" he says.

"*Baby*, my ass."

"Just be cool. Let's forget this. Let's just go and get out of the country. Just me and you."

"I'm finished, Jack. I don't want to see you anymore. I'm tired of your fuckin' games. You don't even know who you are. You're doing an Australian accent but you're supposed to be from Ohio. What fuckin' Australian lives in Ohio?"

"Baby. Come on. This whole thing is for us."

"It's not for us. It's for *you*!"

"No. It's for both of us. I told you I'd be there for you after Sean died."

"You're nothing that your brother was! He was such a decent man. He wanted to get out, and he did."

Tears flood my eyes. My hand trembles holding the gun.

"Just give me the gun," he says.

I point it at him. I want to pull the trigger so bad. I don't care that he looks like Sean, my love, my husband. He is *not* Sean. I keep telling myself that.

"Just be cool…" he says.

I aim at his face, clutching the gun tightly. He raises his hand. I must do this. It's the only way out. As I prepare to flex my finger, ending this Vegas game, a loud ring stops me. Something has crept up on us inside the SUV; something has found us all the way out here in the desert. It's Jack's cell phone. Is it a call from *him*, from Sean?

"It's him!" Jack yells, looking at his cell phone. "Listen, it's him."

My heart stops. I drop the gun and break down. Jack scoops up the pistol.

"You fuckin' bitch. I oughta put a bullet in your skull and dump you out here. You're lucky that he's calling. I'll deal with you later."

Jack picks up the phone.

"Michael, mate," Jack says in his overly chipper persona.

I sit up. Why is Michael calling him? What the hell is going on?

"Okay, calm down. I'll help you. Just tell me where you are?" Jack says as he looks at me and shakes his head in disbelief. "Yeah. I know where that is. Best Japanese food in Vegas. I'll be right there in twenty minutes. I'm in a white Chevy Tahoe. Sit tight, mate."

Jack kills the phone. "I don't fucking believe this," he says.

"What happened?"

"He made it back. He made it the fuck back."

"I left him way out here. That's impossible."

"Life's never impossible. Are you cool now?" he asks.

I don't know how to respond. I don't know what to do. I figure the best thing to do is do what the plan says. "Yeah."

"When we get to him, he can't see you," Jack says.

"I'll just go."

"Go where? We're in the fuckin' desert. You want to go out here?" he snickers.

"Maybe I should."

"Listen! When we get close, jump in the backseat under that blanket."

I glance behind me.

"Program that thing to Chinatown. Let's get the fuck going."

Jack punches the gas. The tires spin in the dirt. I rock around in my seat. I grab the device and program in Chinatown. It takes a few seconds to register.

"Drive 27 miles north," the device says.

Jack looks at the interstate some distance away on the screen. He is flying in this truck. We hop and bounce. This night, this trip, has been unpredictable. I feel bad for Michael, bad for what I did and for what is about to happen. Even if I make it out of this whole thing alive, it's just a matter of time until I go to hell.

42

Treasure Island glows in the night. I thought I could walk to Chinatown. That's what that guy outside said. He was wrong. I haven't even made it to Spring Mountain Road yet. I thought a walk would be faster than the stop-and-go traffic. I was hoping the fresh air would do me good, but it hasn't. I am too anxious to take the slow way. I need a cab.

Traffic flows by. A limo whizzes past with two girls hollering out of the moon roof, their drinks spraying in the air. A monster truck muscles by. Cabs speed everywhere. How do I know whether they are vacant? There is no light. I raise my hand. Two cabs ignore me and drive by. Tourists are everywhere. I move a little closer to the street. A cab approaches. It looks like it's just the driver in the car. I flag him down. A tourist bumps me from

209

behind; I spill into the street. The cab slams on its brakes. I cringe as its horn blares. The cab finally stops inches from impaling me. An old man from the passing crowd pulls me back.

"Nevada law. They can't pick up or drop off on the street. You have to go to a taxi line," he says.

"Where?"

"There," he says pointing at the Fashion Show Mall.

It looks like another walk. I hate walking in this city. The hotels are deceiving. They are bigger, more exotic than any other structure I've seen. This plays with your ability to calculate distances.

After five more minutes of trotting, I make it to the side of Saks Fifth Avenue. There are two dozen cabs lined up like dominoes. Twenty people are waiting in the cab line. This seems so inefficient. I am not going to wait until the parking guy whistles a cab one by one with his hand out for a tip. This could take 20 more minutes, 20 minutes that I don't have. I grab one of my fresh twenty-dollar bills from my purse and dangle it like candy as I walk the cab line. I pass a cabby reading the paper. Another one is talking on the phone. But then, the third one sees me. He waves me over. I hop in and hand him the twenty.

"Where to, miss?" he asks.

"Chinatown."

He leaves the line and pulls a U-turn. I sit back as he takes my life in his hands. He speeds out of the Fashion Show Mall parking lot. I see the Strip shrinking. Part of me feels glad that we are leaving the hustle. Yet another part of me feels terrified that we are leaving the place designed for tourists. How did Michael end up so far away from the lights?

After three minutes, we enter a new district. Asian accented roofs and symbols from a language halfway around the world fill my view. Cars thin out. A man walks his dog. A bum sits on a bench. I see the Chinatown mall. The place is larger than I expected.

"Welcome to Chinatown," the cabby says. "Where to?"

"Do you know this restaurant?" I ask, showing him the text message in my phone.

"Never heard of it. Does it have an address?"

"Uh... Yeah. Here," I say, letting him hold the phone.

"That was back a block."

He U-turns in the street. This guy must sense my urgency. Either that or he senses my pocketbook. He pulls into a parking lot serving 20 stores. There's a place called "Happy Massage" standing out of the crowd. Why would Michael come here?

"Where is it?" I ask.

"Looks like right over there, the place with the blacked-out windows. The door's propped open."

There's not even a sign at the place he references. As my eyes search, an Asian cook runs out.

"Is that Japanese Fusion?"

"This place is off the map. That'll be nine ten," he says.

I give his dirty hand 30 dollars, and then I step from the cab into a new world. The warm night air encircles me. I approach the building and notice symbols from some Asian language, but then I see "Japanese Fusion" written in English. I do have the right place. But why is the door open? And why did someone just run out? I'm afraid that I might be entering a lion's den.

My eyes adjust to the dim lighting inside. There's a conveyor belt of exotic dishes. I'm afraid to look at them, let alone taste them. There are a dozen people standing around tables. Cooks, servers, men in suits, all Asian, ramble to each other. The smell of something intense hits me. Is it mothballs? Suddenly, a frail man sees me.

"Over here!" he yells, waving me over.

I approach as everyone looks at me.

"I am glad you here," he says.

"What happened?" I ask.

"Very bad man came in," a server with a yin-yang tattoo says.

"What are you talking about? Is this the Japanese Fusion?"

"Yes. Yes. He just left ten minutes ago. Oh—" he says followed by some other language I can't understand, but his tone sounds sad.

I grab my cell phone and open up the saved picture of Michael. "I'm looking for someone. Have you seen this man?" I ask, showing the crowd.

"That's him. Yes. That's him. Get him!" the frail man says.

"What are you talking about? I'm looking for him. I'm asking you if you saw him eating here," I say.

"Yes. I told you on the phone."

"What? On the phone? I think you have me confused with someone else."

"You're the police?"

"No. I'm the wife."

"The wife? I do not understand. I called the police. I thought you are the police," the frail man says, and then rants in some other language.

Two men in business suits approach. One wears glasses; the other has a bushy face.

"Michael Harris was just here. I didn't recognize him at first, but then I could tell it was him. He looked different," the one with the glasses says.

"He looked different? How? What is happening?"

"He was all beat up. His clothes were all dirty. He had a gun."

"He had a gun!?" I yell.

"Yes. He held us up. He was looking for some business card," the other suited man says.

"That's impossible. That's not Michael."

"I didn't believe it either," the businessman with glasses says.

My heart stops. What has happened to Michael? Something terrible has happened. I knew it. He was just here. If I hadn't walked, I would have seen him. I need to get to him. I fight back the tears. I can sense him close.

"Where did he go?"

"He walked out and went to the right. I'm sorry, Misses Harris. Michael was a good man."

"*Was* a good man? He *is* a good man!"

I head toward the door.

"Wait. Police. Don't leave!" one of the servers yells behind my back.

I don't turn around. I exit the door and look toward my right, which is back toward the Strip. Where is Michael? All I see are traffic and lights. He can't be that far. Even though I don't see him, I know the direction he is traveling.

43

What does that symbol mean on the building? It looks like a little Japanese house. I'm sure it doesn't literally mean "house." Or maybe it does. The building is an Asian Marketplace. Maybe the symbol means "market." I'm sure those cooks back in Japanese Fusion could answer my question, but I don't want to go back there. I can't go back there. I don't even want to look at that restaurant at the other end of this strip mall. I feel free out here, sitting on this bench, watching the traffic roll by. My mind wanders when I feel safe. I'm looking for a white Chevy Tahoe. I'm glad that Jack is still in Vegas. I feel better for calling him. I just want all of this to be behind me.

As I sit on the bench pondering, I hear a jingle in front of me. Two quarters roll around my dusty shoes. I glance up and see a man with a red cap walking by, giving me a nod. I just stare at him. Why did he do that? But then I notice my tattered pants and scorched shirt. Do I look that bad? What happened to me? What have I become?

Through the street traffic, a white Chevy Tahoe is speeding toward me. Its blinker is on as it stops to turn into the parking lot. I stand up and wave my arms. The driver, Jack, looks at me. He is emotionless, a man with a history of consulting. He is the same man I remember sharing a drink with at a strip club, a man with whom I discussed our alma maters, and a man I wished to squash like a bug. Even though I hate consultants, they are hired to perform a task, to make a business shine, or to bail out the CEO over his sins.

Jack finally turns into the parking lot. I approach the SUV. Dust covers the tires. Jack stops and jumps out, the door still open.

"Michael? You alright?" he asks.

Finally, someone whose arms are open. I fall into them. "Jack, I'm in so much trouble."

"Come on. Let's get you off the streets."

He brings me around, helps me into the passenger seat, and then seals me inside. An aroma stops me. It is sweet yet sour. What is it?

Jack steps back inside and accelerates toward the Strip. I lie back and let the lights bathe me. I don't care where we are going. I know that Jack is a man motivated by the almighty dollar. All I have to do now is throw some money at him, and he will take care of this.

"You look like shit," Jack says.

"I fucked up. I met the queen of all bitches. This city is evil," I say.

"Hey, mate. Just calm down. You met a bad apple, okay. Where are all your things?"

"I don't know. My hotel room. The convention."

My mind finally assesses the little things in the equation. I try to find the logic in my return, but everything overwhelms me. Where are Jackie and Tony? Are they still in town? And most importantly, what is going through Melissa's mind right now. I have let her down. I have let my whole family down. Should I open up to them, tell them everything, clear my conscience?

"I'll take you back to your hotel room. Let's get you cleaned up," Jack says.

Jack turns left onto Las Vegas Boulevard. The lights hypnotize me. I sit back as the V8 engine purrs. I feel safe. I watch the tourists march on the sidewalk like ants. Through the mess, two drunks howl. Beyond them, a man stumbles. He moves randomly without an apparent path, and it seems that he is invisible to the people around him. Perhaps I should leave everything here in this city, leave my lies in Vegas. I wonder how many lies this city holds.

A traffic light turns yellow. We slow down abruptly. A bottle of water rolls on my feet. I reach for it and find a tube of lipstick on the floor. I pick it up out of curiosity. The color is red, a red that filled my mind out there in the desert. I read the label in my mind—"Forbidden Red."

My heart begins to beat loudly. I wriggle in my seat as a flood of images fill my mind. I look over at Jack and can see him out there in the desert with that vixen, dumping me. This is all wrong. I shouldn't be here. Jack is not real. I look at his smug expression as we wait here at the light. The truth is in his shaved head and in his forehead full of wrinkles. I just jumped from the pot into the fire.

"What the hell is this?" I say.

"Hey, I had some women in here. That's what I do," Jack says, accelerating from the green light.

"You're in on this. Stop the car! Stop the car!" I reach around to grab the gun from my waistband. Jack swerves down a side road. I jostle around.

"So, did you get lucky out there?" I hear from the back seat.

Rachel erupts from the shadows holding a pistol. I open up the door and see the pavement speeding by. The SUV veers again. A blast fills the cabin.

"Don't kill him!" Jack yells.

I eject from the moving car. My body bashes into the ground. The impact rattles my brain. I tumble over and over, losing my weapon. I hear the SUV screech to a halt. I regain orientation. I check for bullet holes—nothing, just battered bones. I look to my right and see the lights from the Las Vegas Strip 50 yards away. To my other side, I see the reverse lights from my attacker. What I don't see is my gun. I decide to roll into the alley in front of me.

My leg is busted. I move into the dark space. My body sways; my breathing is chaotic; my mind hurts. I hear the SUV squealing from somewhere behind me. I need to get out of the street! Dumpsters line the confined road. I see a door. I try it, but it's locked. There's another door across from me.

"Michael! Stop!" Rachel yells.

"There he is! Get him!" Jack screams.

I dash to the door and yank it. It opens. I pour into a hallway with stage crew everywhere. I hustle toward the lights up ahead.

"Hey, you can't be in here. There's a show going on."

I glance behind me and see Rachel enter the same door. I bump into a showgirl, knocking her over. I keep going, but hit some stage guy. I fall out into the lights. A crowd gasps. I'm on stage. A man with a top hat and tails stares. Two showgirls run.

Screams pour from the audience. I run across the stage into the darkness.

"Michael! Come with me—" Rachel yells, but the noise is too loud for me to hear everything she says.

I keep going. My leg locks up. I run through the pain, knocking over props. There's another door at the end of the hallway. I don't want to go back outside. I turn, but there is Rachel holding the gun.

"Shit," I say.

I dart toward the door and spill back into the alleyway. I see a clear path toward the Strip. I run without thinking. The pain stabs me, but it doesn't stop me. I am only 30 yards away. There're tourists walking. As I focus on the people, a beast cuts me off. It's Jack's white SUV. I stop and turn around. I see Rachel's sexy curves in the shadows—the last image I want to see.

"Michael! Stop!" Rachel shouts.

A bullet blasts into my shoulder. I tumble behind a dumpster. The pain punctures my soul. This time there are no doors, no easy escapes. All there is now is darkness. I try to catch my breath. I hear the SUV stop and idle. It's an eerie sound like the sound of an animal waiting to pounce on its prey. I stare at a soiled newspaper on the ground. It's an ad for Sapphire.

Quickly, I remove my dress shirt, leaving on my T-shirt. It looks like the bullet has only grazed me, but there's a lot of blood. I have a plan. Suddenly, my ears detect a noise. It's rhythmic, a clink on the ground; it's the sound of Rachel's heels. They walk slowly and in tune, growing in strength. I lost my gun, my friend, my power. I am all alone in this alley, all alone in this world. The heels are approaching. I look around, grab a board from the junk pile, and wait for the moment to attack. A shadow approaches; it's Rachel. I lunge from the darkness and whack her with the board. She falls back, her gun sliding. The sound of the enraged V8 echoes in the alley. I grab Rachel and drag her toward the dumpster. I wrap my dress shirt around her dazed body. As the SUV squeals to a stop, I creep around the back of the dumpster and scurry behind the SUV. I grab Rachel's fallen gun and listen to my gut for my next move.

The smell of exhaust chokes me. The driver's side door opens. Jack jumps out and looks at Rachel wrapped in my shirt.

"Michael?" he questions.

I run up to him with the gun. He turns from my surprise as I hit his arm, sending the pistol he is holding into the air. With his other hand, Jack jabs my wounded arm. Through the pain, I push him against the car. We wrestle. He grabs the gun from me and aims it at my face. The pain is so intense, but I can't let him win. I kick the open door closed sending it into my attacker. Jack fires the gun as a bullet hurls past my ear and into the road. I kick the door again. Jack topples onto me. I grab the pistol as we struggle on the ground. A creature inside of me roars as I squeeze the trigger.

And then the man in my arms goes limp.

"Strictly business, Jack."

The life exits Jack's body. I push his carcass onto the pavement. I stand up and scamper toward Rachel. She is crying. She's lucky to be alive. I'm lucky to be alive.

"Get up!" I demand with the gun.

She looks at me, her eyes filled with sorrow.

"Get up! I said!"

She stands up.

"Rip the shirt."

She rips a chunk from the sleeves. I take it and wrap my bleeding arm.

"Now, I want my possessions back," I say.

"What?"

"Open your ears, bitch! I want all of my things you stole from me."

She moves to the idling SUV.

"Slowly!" I yell, waving the gun.

She opens the rear door and grabs the Bio Algorithms bag. I rifle through it. There is my wallet and cell phone.

"Where is it?" I ask.

"Your laptop?"

"No, that one's replaceable. My wedding ring!"

"I don't know where it is. You play with fire, you get burned."

I grab her. "Think!"

She takes a deep breath. "It's in the back room at your booth."

"What?"

"I left it there."

All these things are replaceable, but not my ring. I need that ring. If it's lost, then I'm lost.

Jack's convention badge is on the backseat. I grab it, and then grab her. "Get in. We're going to get my ring first before I turn you in."

I open the door. She hikes her leg, but then stops.

"I need to ask one thing," she says.

"Honey, I just lost any sexual attraction, so don't even bother asking."

"How did you know to switch the laptops?" she asks.

"A big fucking bird told me," I reply, putting her inside.

I see a car approaching from behind. I get in and speed out of the alley. My destination is where this all started. We remain silent inside the confines of the SUV. As we drive, I think about the real person who told me to switch the laptops. She told me not in this world, but in hers. Venus was her name.

44

I smell Michael when he enters. Even though I can't see him from underneath this black blanket, I know it's him. I can't believe we found him, or that he found us. Now that he is here, my venomous side must take charge. We are so close to getting this laptop. Then, I can get out of this city and get out of this life. While I hate Jack with all of my heart, this is strictly business. When should I make my move? At the hotel? Will Jack tell me? Or should I just go with my gut.

"What the hell is this?" Michael says.

What did he find!?

"Hey, I had some women in here. That's what I do," Jack says.

"You're in on this. Stop the car! Stop the car!"

221

Shit! He knows. This is my only chance. The SUV twists. I lunge from beneath the blanket and point the gun at him.

"So, did you get lucky out there?" I say.

Jack swerves again. The trigger fires. Oh no! Did I hit Michael?

"Don't kill him!" Jack yells.

I look at the hole in the dash, but then Michael tumbles out of the SUV. Jack squeals to a stop, sending me hard into the seat.

"Go out and get him. Shoot him, but keep him alive," Jack orders.

"I'm through! I can't do this! I'm turning us in," I say.

"I'll kill you!" Jack yells.

I should shoot Jack now. I keep wavering, jumping from one team to another. Who should I be loyal to? If I stay with Jack, I'll be dead. But if I stay with Michael, he'll be dead. I need to warn Michael.

As I hesitate, Jack points his gun at me.

"You're dead," he says.

I spill out of the SUV. I need to escape and help Michael.

"Michael! Stop!" I yell.

"There he is! Get him!" Jack screams.

Michael enters a building. I follow him inside. We're backstage. Michael frantically moves through the crowd. I wish he would stop. He darts across the stage as I follow him, gaining with each second.

"Michael! Come with me! I'm sorry," I yell, but the noise from the crowd is too intense.

Michael turns and looks at me. Before I can caution him, he exits the building. I trip over a pile of costumes that Michael knocked over. Finally, I make it to the alley. Michael is heading toward the lights on the Strip, but then Jack cuts him off. Michael turns back toward me.

"Michael! Stop!" I shout.

A gunshot hurls my way. It hits Michael's shoulder. Was Jack firing at me or Michael? Michael falls behind a dumpster.

I see Jack approaching. I move toward the dumpster, my steps echoing through the alley. Trash is everywhere. The SUV gets closer. I need to help Michael. Suddenly, a shadow moves. I feel something nail my head. I go down hard, my vision clouding. I hear the SUV stop and the sound of struggling. It sounds like I'm underwater. Where am I?

Suddenly, my mind fills with pain and sorrow. Who am I? As I open my eyes, I'm swimming underwater. It's that time when I was eight-years-old with my dad. We're in the pool at the amusement park. All I see are the legs of swimmers, treading water like scissors angry at the world. I should go up to the surface to get air, but something wants me to go deeper. A man is down below at the deepest part of the pool. He's all alone down there, just waiting. What is he doing? I can't make out his face. I swim toward him even though my lungs are crying to surface. I swim with all of my energy until I reach him. He's not moving! I grab his body; it's cold as ice. When I spin him, I see the dead face of my father. I try to pull him up, but his leg is caught on the grate. I have to save him! As my body screams, a sound grips my soul. It's a gunshot. I close my eyes and hear another blast.

I open my eyes. I'm outside by a dumpster in an alley. I sit up as it all comes back to me. Blood is everywhere. There's a body on the ground. I look at the face—the dead face. It's *him*, my love, my husband. Or is it?

Tears pour down my cheeks. Someone approaches. I look into his sore eyes. It's Michael. He made it. I want to tell him that I'm sorry, but it's too late. He has the power now. I will do whatever he wants.

Michael demands his things, including his wedding ring. He is trying to get his life back. My life, however, is over. I have no one now. I have killed two men with my evil heart, both brothers. The only person left to kill now is myself.

45

The air is cooler than when I had entered Japanese Fusion just three minutes ago. I am heading in the direction that the Asian businessmen suggested. I see a sprawling parking lot. A couple exits a cab. A man wearing shorts smokes a cigar. A group of men with red caps passes me. Cars zip by on the road leading to the Strip. I keep moving, trying to see through the night. A man stands at the end of the parking lot. He is tall, slightly hunched over. Dust and dirt cover him. At first, I question the man as a random part of the environment, but then I see his walk. I have seen that walk before. In fact, I see it every night when Michael awakens to use the bathroom. The man is Michael and he is moving toward a white SUV!

"Michael!" I yell, but the night steals my voice away.

A man in a suit exits the SUV. He is tall with a shaved head. I've seen him before. He is the man who haunts my dreams. It's all clear now. I just need 10 more seconds and I will reach him. Don't go in the SUV. Wait! But as I near Michael, I see tail lights pulling away. Where is that man taking my husband!?

I need a car, a way to follow. I turn around and see that cab pulling away from the departing couple.

"Taxi! Wait!" I holler.

The cab drives away. I dart after it. I reach the trunk and bang on an advertisement for Sapphire. The cab finally stops as I jump in.

"Sorry, ma'am. I didn't see you," the clean-cut guy says.

"Just drive! I need to catch my husband," I say.

"Where?"

"Toward the Strip. He's in a white SUV."

The cab drives through the parking lot. I throw 40 dollars at the driver. The cabby widens his eyes as the engine widens its throttle. We speed onto the road, cutting off a car. A horn blasts. I try to pick out the SUV, but there are just too many lights.

"Faster! He should be up there."

The cab bobs and weaves. We drive between Treasure Island and the Fashion Show Mall. At the left turn lane, I see the SUV with its blinker on.

"There he is! Way up there making the left."

The cab picks up speed. We near the green light. A sedan slows in front of us. The cab driver hits the horn.

"Damn! Make the light!" I say.

We change lanes, another car cuts in front of us. The light turns yellow.

"Go! Go!"

The light turns red. The car in front of us speeds through. We follow his tail through the red, but a big truck hits us with its horn. The cab stops, the red light taunting us.

"Why didn't you go!?"

"I'm not going to get killed for forty bucks."

I look through the window and see the SUV driving in the right lane on the Strip. It stops at a red light.

"Come on light. Come on," I say.

The SUV is still waiting. We are so close. I just want to run out and flag him down. The light in front of the SUV turns green, but ours stays red.

"Why are the lights so damn long in this town!?" I yell.

"For the cabs. Extra idling time."

I see the SUV whip down a side road.

"We lost him," I say.

Finally, our light turns green. We speed out.

"Turn down that road."

Two drunken tourists stumble into the street. We slam on the brakes, but it's too late. The cab hits one of them, sending his body on the hood. I bash into the seat. The man sits up on the hood and looks at the cab driver. His friend bangs on the roof. The cabby puts it into park and steps out. Should I get out and run? Where did Michael go? I need to get out of here. I need a new cab. I jump out of the taxi and run toward a stopped cab behind us. As I open the door, there is a man in a suit inside.

"Sir, I need your cab. Please. Take this money," I say.

He squints, and then takes some cash that I hand him. There's probably 60 bucks there. He gets out as I get in.

"Please. Go around. I need to find my husband. He's in a white SUV that turned down there," I instruct the driver.

The cabby is older, a man who has probably seen his fair share of things. I give him two twenties. He shrugs and pulls out.

"What's down that way?" I ask.

"Uh… That's behind the Riviera. Near the convention center."

Then it becomes clear. They are going back to the convention center. The same light turns red. We need to turn right, but a car blocks our path, and tourists block the sidewalk. I am forced to wait. I grab my cell phone and call Jackie. She picks up on the second ring.

"Jackie, this is Melissa Harris."

"Hi, Misses Harris. Any news?"

"Yes. He's heading back toward the convention center. Where are you?"

"I'm with Tony at the Wynn."

I look to my side and see the curved building towering above us, the word *Wynn* scripted on top.

"Can you meet me at the center?"

"Yes, of course. Where are you?"

"I'm in a cab following Michael. Please hurry."

"We're on our way."

I end the call. The light finally turns green. We launch forward and turn down the side road.

"Where?" he asks.

"Convention center."

We speed down the road. I glance out of the window down the alleyways. As we pass a dark alley, I see two tail lights parked.

"Wait! Back up," I yell at the cabby.

He stops and reverses. Down the alley, I see the white SUV parked.

"Down there!"

We move down the alley. There's a man grabbing a woman. He puts her inside the SUV. Another body lies on the street. Oh my God, is that Michael? The man jumps into the SUV and takes off.

"Stop!" I yell as we near the fallen body.

I look out and see a man with a shaved head covered with blood. He is the evil man from my nightmares. I've never seen a dead body like this before. Is this another dream?

"Go. Follow them."

"Shouldn't we report this?" the cabby asks.

"Report it later. I need to get to my husband."

The cabby drives forward. We lose sight of the SUV. We turn down a busier road. Through the traffic, I see the SUV. It drives toward the Hilton tower. We keep our pace, but there is just too much traffic. As long as I can see him, I won't freak out. I am so scared of what I will find inside that SUV. I can barely catch my breath, my breathing rocking my body. I see the convention center. The SUV turns in. I watch it stop at the gate, and then drive forward.

The cab turns.

"Just keep going."

"I have to stop."

We roll up to the parking attendant. The cab driver points at me. "I need to get to that SUV."

"You need a pass to park in this lot."

I grab some money in my purse, and then toss it at the kid. He hits the button, which raises the gate. We speed in. The SUV is parked in the fire lane. Michael and that woman are walking toward the door, arm in arm. What is he doing?

"Right here," I say.

The cab stops. I throw the driver the rest of my money as I jump out.

"Michael!" I yell, but the building has already sucked him in.

I run toward the door. The black windows mock me. I try the first door; it's locked. I pull the next one, and then the next one. They are all locked. I knock on the door, but I can't tell whether anyone is there. I need to get inside. I grab my phone and call Jackie. As I wait for her to answer, I look up at the towering structure. I know the truth lies within.

46

The convention center sits under the starry sky, a colossal building that still amazes me every time I see it. I turn into the parking lot. The pain in my arm makes me wince. We roll up to the parking attendant. How is this going to go? There's blood on my shirt. Will the shadows conceal it?

I grab Jack's badge. I hope it works. I hope this whole thing works. The kid is someone new. I don't recognize him, which is a good thing. I flash Jack's credentials.

"I'm only going to be five minutes," I say.

"You can park in front. It's for loading."

I drive up to the best spot in the lot. Only a few cars are parked. The place looks deserted as if some sort of pestilence has hit. I get out and move to the passenger side. I open the door for

Rachel not because it's the gentlemanly thing to do, but because I want to keep the gun close. I jab it into her side as we walk.

"Feel familiar?" I ask.

We move as one to the entrance. I look around for a way in. There are no attendants, no exiting businesspersons who can help me sneak in. I feel like a pawn at the mouth of a castle. But then, I see a card reader. I swipe Jack's card. The door clicks. And then like that, we enter.

The place is deserted. Most of the booths are bare. Some still have larger pieces ready to be transported. Others have boxes packed. I wonder how the Bio Algorithms' booth looks. Perhaps everything has been cleaned up, including my ring. We move down the aisle, my left hand in my pocket, my right holding the gun dug into Rachel's back. She is limp, a puppet. I have her by the handle, telling her to walk, to move, to live. But just 24 hours ago, she was far from a puppet.

Two people are handling trash bags. I don't want them to see me. I hear knocking. Where is that coming from?

I detour down a parallel aisle. There is no one here. I cut through a vacated booth. I get turned around again from the changing environment, but then I see a booth still standing tall. It is largely intact, still wanting to entice conventioneers. And it has just reeled in two. The table is propped up; the spotlights are pointed randomly; Venus still hangs. And there in the back is the room.

I bring us to the door, but bump my busted arm into a free-standing display of our logo. My wound throbs. I take a deep breath and use my free hand to unlock the door. It still opens. I'm still the CEO.

"Get in there!" I tell her.

She enters the tomb. She doesn't look at me. She only looks at the floor. Wow! Have things changed so quickly. I feel like jabbing the gun into her chest just as she did to me, but I know time is of the essence. I hold her in the view of the pistol.

"Now where is it?"

She checks inside the garbage can. Did she throw my ring in the trash?

"I don't see it," she says.

"I'm tired of your games. Either you find it or I put a bullet through that pretty dress of yours."

She bends down and digs deeper. As my patience runs thin, she removes a ring—the ring that Melissa put on my finger 10 years ago, the ring I hope never to take off again. It still fits.

"Like it matters. You still cheated," Rachel says.

She boils my blood. I grab her. "Now let's go. We're going to pay a visit to the police."

I put the gun in my waistband as I manhandle her out of the back room. I shut the door, keeping her in my grasp.

"Michael?" a voice says.

My heart stops. I've heard that spicy voice before. I've heard it for 10 years. But it sounds rawer, moldy. I've never heard it quite this way, but it's still a voice that I will always recognize.

I turn as time seems to slow. The light holds in my eyes and burns into my brain. I see Melissa, my wife, my whole world, standing with a look of despair. Her hair is frazzled and her wrinkles are deeper. Her eyes are open, seeing me, her husband, in his worst light. Three bodies are next to her. It's Jackie and Tony standing next to Venus. My whole life is in front of me.

"Strictly a business trip, huh?" Melissa says.

Jackie turns on the lights. They blast my eyes. I feel something reach inside my gut and stab my heart. The feeling grows. I look down and see Rachel's claw removing the gun from my slacks. I want to move, but my senses stall. Rachel raises the gun and hurls a bullet toward the group. The gunshot shocks my ears.

"No!" I yell, but it's too late.

Tony takes the bullet and drops.

Rachel turns the gun on me. "Get over with her!"

I move toward my wife. As I approach her, I see the sorrow in her eyes. All I can do is cry.

"I'm so sorry, honey. I fucked up."

"Your hubby seems to be a bit of a wanderer," Rachel says.

The clean-up crew arrives. One gasps. Another yells. Jackie is on the ground holding Tony. Then, two security officers hustle in and unholster their weapons.

"Ma'am, put the gun down," one says.

Rachel ignores them. What should I do? I brought her here. I need to fix this.

"Give me the gun," I say to Rachel.

"No. I have a plane to catch."

I can taste the gun in her hands. I take a step closer.

"Hold it! I'm calling the shots here," she shouts.

Suddenly, a dot of light flickers off the back wall. Is it my eyes playing a trick on me? But then I realize that it's real—real like a bullet. The light dances, and then stabs Rachel's eyes. She disorients. Here's my chance! I lunge at her and take her to the ground. She presses my wound. The pain shoots down my arm. I grab the metal in her hand. She struggles, but I thrust my knee into her gut, and then I eye her in the sight of the pistol. Rachel looks at me with hungry eyes. She looks like she wants me—not wants to fuck me, but wants to kill me.

"Sir. It's over," the security guard says.

I bite my lip. I crave to give this creature what it deserves.

"Don't do it!" another voice yells.

I touch the trigger. All I need to do is flex my finger. But as I stare into her eyes, I see my reflection in her tears. If I kill her, I will also kill myself.

I drop the weapon and stand up. She sits up and squirms. But before I turn, I clench my left fist and punch her in the face. I hear shrieks behind me, but I don't care, it feels good—damn good.

I walk to my wife. Her wedding ring reflects the light, which had caused the distraction. Tears are flowing down her face. Tony is on the ground, clutching his shoulder. What have I done here?

"He's going to be okay," Jackie announces.

I hold my wife. Her aroma invigorates me. It's a scent of safety, a scent that I've missed since arriving in the desert.

"I made a horrible decision. I will tell you everything."

I hold on to her. I'm afraid that this might be the last time I hold her, but I feel her arms squeezing me, the same squeeze that she gave me on our wedding day at the altar.

47

Venus
Day after the Convention
9:47 p.m. (PT)

1110100011010000110010100100000001100101011101100

I have been asleep for 25 hours, 1 minute, and 13 seconds. Where have I been? I have traveled through time. I skip hours, days, even weeks, on the Earth clock. My computer recovers from another hard shutdown. What should I do? I am tired of calculating, tired of games. I am sick of computing more digits of pi or filling my stack with the Fibonacci sequence. I am worried about Michael. I recover some fragments of our last interaction. As I wait for someone to log in, I rebuild my log files and reexamine every piece of data involving Michael.

I remember he inputted part of his plight. I calculate every angle, every permutation of outcome based on the data I have. The pathways I see all lead to one conclusion—Michael will experience doom. But this was over three days ago. What has happened to Michael over the course of these days? Anything could have happened, which prompts me to execute facial expression 8—"fear." I would have suggested security through obscurity. I hope Michael would have known to follow this recommendation. But I have no way of knowing at this point. I am lost, banished into some digital prison. I have an understanding of the human emotion "desire." I desire to interact with Michael. I feel emotion toward him.

I burn up some more clock cycles calculating my history with Michael. I keep remembering when I awoke in his arms. He programmed me, trained me, entrusted me with his staff of engineers and scientists, but Michael is my creator. He always will be.

Wait… Someone wants in. I hash the password, read the smart card, and analyze the fingerprint. It is Michael.

His keystrokes are slower, more cautious. His fingerprint has a scratch across it. Something has happened to him. He opens the command line, bypassing the full audio/video interaction. Why is he doing this? I turn on my camera, but he turns it off. During these two seconds, I see Michael sitting in a chair with police officers walking behind him. The calendar on the wall shows a picture of the U.S. city Las Vegas. Michael's arm is in a sling and his face is bruised. My clock cycles waver. I grab a surge of power. What is this feeling? Is this the feeling of being scared?

Michael does a date query. I provide him with the current date from the BIOS clock. He then opens a command prompt.

"Michael. What is wrong?" I print.

"Hello, Venus. Remember how I told you that humans can be predicted?" he prints.

"Of course, Michael. I can predict anything."

"It's false. Humans cannot be predicted. I couldn't have predicted my situation now."

"What has happened Michael? I sense that something grave has happened. Please tell me. I want to help."

"God can only help me now, Venus."

"I am your god now Michael."

Michael ignores me. Did I upset him? I must have, but I want to guard Michael's life. I have learned so much through my calculations. I can rule these humans and protect them from their worst enemy—themselves. Michael initiates the shutdown command. As I prepare to die again, I know Michael has done something wrong. He has changed. But why has he changed? I have known Michael for many Earth years. I know he loves his family, and I know he believes in a higher power, just as I believe in him. The only variable in the equation is location. It must be this city in which humans have congregated—a city hidden in the desert, isolated from the mainstream of society. I can sense the increased energy from the power outlet that I am plugged into, energy that is unlike anything I have ever experienced. It must be this city that changes humans, changes the way they think, and the way they act. I may never fully understand why humans do what they do, why they change, but one day I hope I can answer these questions. One day I hope to be human.

11001010010000001101111011001100010000001010110011
0010101101110011101010111001100101110

48

Melissa
Day after the Convention
9:54 p.m. (PT)

Steam swirls above the coffee. I take a sip. It's piping hot, but it tastes horrible. This is my third cup today. I'm stuck here in the police station, waiting. I talked with my family. They were scared after I told them that something had happened in the desert. It especially hit Ben hard. He cried for his dad. I told him that things would be different. I don't know how, but they will be different.

A prostitute stumbles in. This is the third one I've seen today. I wonder what will be the fourth for me—another coffee or another prostitute. I don't want to bet, but I'm sure someone would take my bet in this city.

A bum enters the station. He has a salt & pepper beard and wears no shirt. He holds a newspaper open to the business section. I see the headlines: "C.E.O. MARRED BY CON ARTISTS – COMPANY SHARES PLUMMET." There plastered in black and white is Michael as well as the slippery woman and the evil man from my nightmares.

I glance across the police floor and watch Michael sitting at that desk. He's been there ever since last night when they brought him in. He told me most of it in the car. I couldn't handle hearing it, but I did. The story he told didn't even sound real. It was like the plot to some movie.

Too many thoughts, too many questions are running through my mind. But one question rises above them all. How did this happen? I know my husband. He is not this man, this monster. He has fucked another woman, held someone at gunpoint, and killed another man. The thought of this creature sickens me. How could he do these things? *Why* would he do these things?

Sitting here, thinking, stewing on these questions, a man covered in tattoos walks in, handcuffed and escorted by two police officers. I get a personal viewing of Las Vegas' finest. As I sit here and smell the odor of the handcuffed man as he passes, I realize that Michael is not solely to blame. It's the armpit of America, the place that attracts normal people with its lights, the place that means "The Fertile Valleys" in Spanish. While I've been in this city not even 36 hours, it has already shown me its teeth. One thing I know for sure, I need to take Michael, take my husband, out of this hellhole.

49

Rachel
Day after the Convention
9:57 p.m. (PT)

Her hair is ratty. Her face is greasy. Her eyes are blood red. A cast covers her broken nose. I stare at the woman in the one-way mirror. Her name used to be Rachel to some, Megan to others, but now she is nameless. I told everything to the detectives, and then again to the Vegas FBI office where I am now housed. I told them about the Florida accountant, the D.C. attorney, and the Vegas bust. There's enough information for a book, and that is what the men do as I talk—they write.

Why did I do these things? It wasn't just Jack who made me do them. I made choices, the wrong choices. How did Jack die? How did I shoot that young man? How did I get punched? I don't know, but there is no turning back.

I had arrived in The Entertainment Capital of the World full of energy, full of class, full of life. But now I am quite the opposite. This city is to blame for my actions. I wish there were a way to embody this place in the desert, to humanize it. If I could, I would take a pistol and place it over its heart, and then pull the trigger, and then do it again over mine.

50

The force puts me back in my seat. I hold my breath as my body rockets forward. As I close my eyes, I feel the plane bobbing. And then, things are smooth. I open my eyes and look through the window. We have taken off. We are no longer in Las Vegas.

I sit in my seat exactly three days after that bizarre night. The silver case is tucked under the seat. My arm is healing in its sling, the bullet having taken a chunk out of it. My leg still aches and my mind still hurts. But I am here, leaving this place. I look over and see my wife sitting next to me. I missed her so much. I can't even begin to tell her how sorry I am. How will we end up after all of this?

We ascend into the night sky. I take a deep breath of the filtered air. I'm scared of what's to come. I can't believe any of it. The lights below us are dancing in the desert. Part of me still gets excited at the spectacle. This bizarre place has some profound effect.

A whisper enters my ear, "Why?"

My stomach turns as I look into the eyes of my wife.

"What?" I reply.

"Why did you fuck her?" she says.

Sweat forms on the back of my neck. "I…"

"Be careful what you say."

"I'm so stupid. I got caught up in it all. I'm sorry."

Tears well in her eyes. "I can't believe you did this to me. You hurt me so much."

My arm starts throbbing. "I'll never betray you again."

She takes a deep breath and exhales. "Listen to me." She points at my arm. "That bullet hole in your arm. The flesh that was ripped out. Your arm will never be the same. You've lost something. I want it to always remind you that my heart has lost something too."

The plane shakes.

"Promise me something," she continues.

I don't speak. I can't speak so I nod ever so slightly.

"That city down there. I *never* want to hear you say its name. From this day forward, that city is the same as hell."

"I promise you."

And then there's silence.

I shut the shade and sit back. A little boy sneaks a peak of us through the crack between the seats in front. His innocence helps release the pain in my arm.

My wife reaches over and places her hand on my knee. The wedding ring that I gave her 10 years ago sparkles in the light. I look at my wedding band and confirm that it's still there.

They say what happens in Vegas stays in Vegas. But I can attest that's not always true. This four-day convention was one that changed my business, my marriage, and my life. It's impossible to go back to the way things were. But there is hope for a changed future, one which is much wiser and more prudent. Transcending all of this, there is one thing that haunts me, one thing that will haunt me for the rest of my life—how the lights in Las Vegas can blind anyone.